FABRICATIONS

FABRICATIONS

ADAM MARS-JONES

ALFRED A. KNOPF NEW YORK 1981

The author would like to make it known that in his research for the story
"Bathpool Park" he found particular assistance in the full and
well-documented account of the Neilson case, *The Capture of the Black
Panther,* by Harry Hawkes (London: Harraps, 1978).

Library of Congress Cataloging in Publication Data
Mars-Jones, Adam, [date] Fabrications.
Contents: Hooshmi—Bathpool Park.
1. Mars-Jones, Adam, [date] Bathpool Park.
1981. II. Title.
PR6063.A659H6 1981   823'.914   81-47514
ISBN 0-394-51998-1   AACR2

Manufactured in the United States of America

FIRST AMERICAN EDITION

This book is for Mike,
who didn't mean to help.

CONTENTS

H O O S H - M I

A F A R R A G O
O F S C U R R I L O U S
U N T R U T H S
(1 9 7 7)

C H A P T E R

O N E

The great vespertilionid moved silently through the night air, delicately angling the leading edge of its patagium with an occipitopollicalis contraction, and a slight lowering of its thumbs. . . .

You have to go back all the way to the Council of Trent, and the events befalling Cardinal Crescence the Papal Legate, for a reasonably close parallel; or at least as far as 1819, when the Duke of Richmond, Governor-General of Canada, found himself faced with a similarly unfortunate set of circumstances.

A search for less specialised precedents would yield the more familiar names of Fritz, at Camberley, 1969, and Sessan at Newmarket in 1970.

However, had the specimen of <u>lasiurus cinereus</u> which opens our story been possessed of human mentation, it would hardly have been contemplating these melancholy case-histories. It would have been glowing with legitimate pride in its achievements; it had after all very recently confirmed a conjecture made by Mr. A. D. Irvin, M.A., Vet.M.B., M.R.C.V.S., and reported by him in the Veterinary Record for 1970 (number 87, page 333).

Mr. Irvin's article discusses amongst other topics the possible migration from the United States to this country of American hoary bats, which are quite outstandingly strong fliers. In spite of a likely record from the Orkneys, Mr. Irvin doesn't feel able to commit himself positively; nor from P.O. Kabete, Kenya, where he works for the East African Veterinary Research Organisation, can he see with his own eyes the doughty voyager now cruising on the pungent airs of late September just east of Braemar, Aberdeenshire, in its last few hours of health before a unique side-effect of bat physiology lays it low.

For it isn't any longer possible to put a brave face on things; lasiurus' migratory exploit was unintentional, not in the least a scheduled flight. The spatial skills of bats are considerable, but not unlimited; and this specimen had just got lost. Following winds had made possible its arrival in Scotland, but really drowning might have been better, harsh as that verdict sounds.

Bats have a stock of brown fat, the "interscapular gland," stored in their shoulders, which serves them as a reserve energy supply. They can use it as a starter-motor, to initiate their awakening from hibernation; or they can call on it in emergencies, as our bat certainly did on its record-breaking flight.

It's only fair to say that you wouldn't need these nature-notes if you were reading *Jaws;* the moment you have heard the name of the Great White Man-Eating Shark, you have a behavioural model of its dietetic ecology. You can understand its first snack of the book without a field-guide. The hoary bat responds less well to this treatment.

The only disadvantage of brown shoulder fat is a malign counterpart of the slick mechanism which allows bats of many species to mate in October (say) and start hibernation in December, but delay ovulation and conception until next morning (until March): rabies virus can survive in the fat for long periods, only multiplying and making an overt appearance after stress.

And even this isn't so terrible; you could argue that it's

better to slow rabies down, however feebly, than to give in to it right away.

In any case, viral jet-lag is the explanation for lasiurus' decline from health; so that the next dawn but one found it lying on its back in thick bracken, its jaws open to their widest, all but paralysed and nearing death, at the point most easily expressed as Lat. 57°01' N, Long. 3°16' W.

If only the members of the Aberdeenshire and District Natural History Society, as cheery a crowd as you could hope to meet, with their fieldglasses and their thermos flasks, had found it there! They would have given it a place in the Society's display cabinet and in history. It could have relied on having its route endlessly argued over, its age conjectured, the contents of its stomach microscopically analysed. Instead the sole European specimen of the American hoary bat came under the eyes, equally observant but less knowledgeable, of Evesham Pontius Meggezone III.

Pontius made a routine dog reconnaissance, snuffling absorbedly around the area which had attracted his attention. Unable to identify the smell-images so far received, he then prodded the weakly palpitating stomach with his nose. The bat made no response until the moist black bulb of nose came within reach of its just mobile jaws. It bit down firmly, and wasn't at once dislodged by the dog's frantic shakings and pawings. Deliverance in fact came only when Pontius' mistress, not far off but screened from sight by the dense bracken, whistled with her usual piercing volume to call him home.

With one inspired shake Pontius flung off the bat, now as limp as a dead leaf, and rushed to join her.

"Hullo Punch here Punchie," she murmured in greeting, smiling down at him and briskly fondling the backs of his ears. Her familiar biped smells were suddenly dear to him; she was altogether a welcome sight, from print headscarf to thick stockings and low-heeled shoes.

After a few moments ritually displaying her affection, she set off for home at the forced-march pace which could be relied on to exhaust any friend or guest who ventured to accompany her; Pontius for once following closely at her heels, mindful for a little while of the dangers of straying too far.

Pontius saw his mistress hardly at all over the next fortnight; he wasn't singled out from the others for a solo walk again, and so saw only her legs with any regularity, from the dogs' privileged position under the dining-table. When she next properly took notice of him, it was in the great dim hall, where he was irritably cuffing at his sore nose and shuffling backwards and forwards on the floor. In the uncertain light the Queen had the sudden horrifying impression that Punchie was paying an absurd homage, retreating backwards before her and making one formal bow after another. This mirage struck her as horrifying because of the special position the pet dogs occupied in her life. With her family of course Her Majesty had an abundantly loving relationship, but that was in part a solidarity natural to people who were all making the best of the same bad job.

(In previous, less regimented reigns, monarchs had engaged in family quarrels just like ordinary people; but for the Windsors a generation gap was a luxury they simply could not afford.)

Her feeling for her dogs was different. She loved them, purely and without limit, for their ignorance of her status; the eyes which gazed up at her as she mashed processed fodder with a hallmarked fork could never be clouded by the thought that she wasn't theirs alone. That she had to be shared with so many million others.

However many Sundays the dogs see their mistress preparing for church, they will never come to guess that the diminutive woman, hardly even a flyweight, so tensely inspecting her appearance in the mirror, is uniquely and By the Grace of God Defender of the Faith.

Who is there to tell them that the hostess who somehow musters obliging interest in the technicalities of shooting, is Colonel-in-Chief of the Malawi Rifles?

And how can they know that the homebody who curls up at her ease on a sofa and sings breathily along with "People Will Say We're in Love," her very favourite tune, has degrees in music from the universities of London and Wales?

Freedom of the Drapers' Company hasn't spoiled her, nor has her incomparable wardrobe made her vain and luxury-loving; but her dogs see nothing of that. They see only her tweeds as rough as emery-boards, the preferred dowdiness of her private life.

All her honours and titles, from the Supreme Governorship of the Church of England to the Elephant of Denmark, are as nothing to her pets; and she relishes their unforced bad nature with unfailing eagerness and pleasure.

Santa Claus conspires yearly with her, to fill the corgis' individual stockings with chocolate drops, and rubber bones.

Enormously relieved that the dog hadn't after all guessed her secret identity (which couldn't be hidden as easily as Clark Kent's), Elizabeth Windsor padded in stockinged feet across the thin carpeting to her pet. She picked him up and made much of him, pressing him to her without particularly noticing the way he wriggled, in his discomfort.

"Punchieluvvamummaduzzie?" she inquired dreamily. "Punchieluvvamummie?" In a gallant and uncharacteristic effort to give pleasure Punchie unrolled a red carpet of distended tongue, and drew it painfully once or twice across his mistress' smiling muzzle.

Annual Dinner of the Republican Society. Speaker, Dr. John Bull.

DR. BULL: The title of my talk tonight is "Royalty and the

Unreal." For if you give the subject a few moments' thought, you will appreciate how contradictory are the demands we make of our ruling family.

The majority of us think that the Royal Family should be "more like ordinary people"; but we also feel, in about the same numbers, that the Queen and her family are denied their right to a private life, and should be left more to their own devices. In this context we expect to have it both ways, with bizarre effects on the House of Windsor. We are confused, and we confuse the objects of our expectations.

I assume everyone here is familiar with the deep trance state which characterises royalty on parade. The Queen Mum, when shown the exact spot in a factory where nineteen workmen had been killed by a bomb, said "Poor things" and walked on, without deviating for a moment from her impersonation of a church-going chocolate-box.

She had nothing to gain by attending more closely; the most imperceptible flickerings of personality would in any case be invested by the public with charm and significance. In her time she has received bouquets of flowery prose simply for giving a hoarse seaman a throat-lozenge; every triviality is seized on as richly characteristic of a grand old lady. All the poor thing can do is submit to her role as a photogenic zombie, steering through life her paralysing aura.

The Queen herself is capable of feats of sleepwalking at least as impressive as her mother's. At an agricultural show in New Zealand, one exhibitor laid his own forty-yard stretch of red carpet at an angle to the official one marking the route of the Queen's tour. Both Queen and Duke on this occasion jumped the points and trundled down the unauthorised line in their usual gracious coma; only when they ended up inspecting a two-room holiday chalet not listed on their schedule did they so much as stir in their sleep.

Prince Philip has more than once commented that in his job

it is better to bore than to offend, which makes a neat reversal of my priorities as an entertainer; but in fact we can improve on the accuracy of his statement. In his job he can either fall short of people's expectations or be taken utterly for granted; he can never take anyone pleasurably by surprise. He can never be plus, only minus or zero; and it is hard to say which is worse. The Queen discovered this sad truth when she tried her hand at light-hearted banter on a visit to Niagara Falls:

"It looks rather damp," she ventured.

But then, seeing that her guides were shattered by this failure to go through the motions, she pulled herself together with an emphatic:

"but it's magnificent!"

Translation into print isn't kind to such attempts at humour; the more sociable component of the comic impulse presupposes or seeks to establish relationships of approximate intimacy and equality, while its less positive aspect, as a mechanism of defence, excludes, wins round, or scores off potential enemies. On neither level can strangers and oppressors like ourselves expect to get the joke.

The royalty literature, to give it a dignified name, retaliates by accompanying every reported witticism with shrieks of canned laughter. So Prince Philip has on top of everything else to bear seeing references to his "famous instant wit, not to be taken seriously, intended as joke," and poor Elizabeth has her every sally crucified in the same way: "Amused herself by the obvious incongruity of the situation, she faked a hobble, clapped a hand to her back, and feigned a mock wince. 'It's me poor back,' she lamented, jokingly."

It is only on the surface that the Royal Family is at all backward-looking or conservative; in reality, its members are faced with such a flood of bogus information from the world and from its media that their attempts to make sense of their lives could hardly be more contemporary. Perhaps in fact their predicament looks forward to the future, to a time when the advertised global village turns out to be a single overlit hall of mirrors.

Supposing, Madame Chairman, that the Grill Room of a hotel which you had just left became the scene of a terrorist outrage, you would be taken aback by headlines of the MRS. RICE IN HOTEL DRAMA variety. But someone like Prince Philip has long since had to adjust to a world which gives back to him only meaningless images, of this and many another sort.

The House of Windsor, in other words, far from providing the once-touted New Elizabethan Era with its instigators and figureheads, has supplied the nation with a pet herd of sacrificial victims. The position of the present ruling family is clearly extreme, and the remarks I hope to make over the next few minutes will apply mainly to this special case; but you may care to reflect on the last time you heard a pop star saying that his new record is his best yet, or the last time you saw a minister defending Government policy on television. On these occasions it is in effect the job talking, with minimal reference to the person who happens to hold it. To be sure, the confusions are immeasurably greater in the case of someone who didn't even choose the job, but only inherited it or contracted a marriage with it, and is still less able to determine where the person ends and the fact takes over; but the similarity is there, in the implication that the media, far from liberating and enriching our possibilities as it once seemed evident that they would, have ended up by paralysing and by impoverishing us.

Let me give you some snapshots of our present Queen's childhood and development. In a touching effort to enable her to mix informally with girls of her own age, the Princess' parents set up, when she was ten or so, the 1st Buckingham Palace Company of Girl Guides. At its first meeting, all the tiny Ladies and Honourables turned up in their smartest frocks and gloves, their heads chock-a-block beneath the ringlets with

briefings from parents and nannies on how to comport themselves In The Presence.

The Princess wasn't impressed. *"They* won't be able to roll
about and get dirty," she jeered.

But this sort of independence and knowledge of her own
mind was never really Elizabeth's forte, and an upbringing
oppressive in its emphasis on duty taught her more and more
to suppress any desires she might have, in the interests of
others. Training began early; when she was hardly past her first
birthday, Alah Knight had worked overtime to coax her into
greeting her parents, returning from a 1927 Commonwealth
tour, with a burbled "Mother." No wonder her father's pet
Australian parrot, with its endless raucous cry of "Jimmie-have-
a-drink," had such a powerful fascination for her.

The distress which male members of her family tended to
express in the form of furious temper manifested itself quite
differently in her case. Even a game like Demon Pounce,
guaranteed to make the serenest nun sick with rage and blood-
lust, drew no spark of temper from her; instead she apologised
for any remotely astute or relevant manoeuvre.

Whereas her father had as a child pulled in fury at a German
master's beard, the young Princess, when flustered by French
verbs, poured ink over her own head in a spectacularly intro-
verted gesture of misery. A sort of tense wretchedness has been
characteristic of her expression ever since; a reasonable enough
facial reaction to her fate of being simultaneously inflated and
squeezed flat.

She took refuge in a grotesque dutifulness and sense of order,
seeking independence of a sort by staying well within the
narrow confines allotted her. This led her at the age of fourteen
into the little obsession of getting out of bed to set her shoes
straight or to refold her clothes. Any decent child psychologist
(had such things been available at the time) would surely have
pounced on her habit of folding up and hoarding the ribbons

from chocolate-boxes. Her insistence, when the sirens sounded, on getting properly dressed before making her way to the shelter in Windsor dungeons seemed so dangerous to her elders that they equipped her and her sister with siren suits to slip into, and miniature suitcases all packed and ready for emergencies.

The main result of Lilibet's retreat into convention was to make Margaret think of her as a Sobersides—a mild enough sobriquet, but hardly likely to make her lot easier to bear.

She was fortunate indeed not to inherit that freakish formation of the ears which had earned her father his school nickname of "Bat Lugs."

Princess Elizabeth's attempt to get on top of her job by welcoming duty with open arms, and excelling by sheer will-power, was doomed from the start; for there was no substance to what was demanded of her, as well as no limit. The genuineness of her sense of duty isn't the point here; even supposing that beneath her icy exterior there hangs a sincere heart of scalding meringue, that her inner life is that of a Baked Alaska in reverse, her subjects cannot in the nature of things gain access to it. She would have done better to accept whole-heartedly that royalty was show business rather than Real Life.

There has always been ample evidence of this—we might remind ourselves that a good many royal coaches and carriages were sold off to Sir Alexander Korda some time before 1952, so that five two-pair broughams and two open landaus had to be borrowed back from his studios, for the Coronation spectacular.

And who after all can determine which of the Queen's regular appointments, the Tuesday evenings with the Prime Minister or the Monday afternoons with the hairdresser (her groomings political or frankly cosmetic), has the greater effect on the running of her country? Had she scrutinised her position more closely, she would have been on her way to resolving the contradictions of her life and resisting its pressures; just as she has developed a purely token handshake and wave to save her from pain and fatigue—thus turning to advantage the fact that in royalty's case these gestures are not expressions of personality, and don't need to be either vigorous or sincere.

P A R T

T W O

It was a mistake on the part of the welcoming committee to have arranged a band of pipers at Sydney airport ready for the royal touchdown.

A little more research would have tipped them off to the Queen's custom of being greeted by the bagpipes at every breakfast-time. Her self-control is a byword, but is naturally unable to override habits and connections established without her conscious participation. Her Majesty could therefore rally her facial muscles into a pose of frozen grimness, but could do nothing about the conditioned reflexes which prompted her stomach to rumble with sudden thunder. The boiling and thrashing of her thwarted juices was quite clearly heard, even during the music, for some distance across the tarmac.

The innocent perpetrator of this gastric outrage was eventually cajoled by her husband into seeing the funny side of the incident; many times in the past a small disaster had actually helped to relieve the tension.

Philip had always made it his business to mediate between the Queen's stiffness and the social demands of the job. If she was uncomfortable in company, he might suggest The Name Game, which always put her at her ease: guests would be told of a recent arrival in the royal stables, and details of its lineage.

Then they would be invited to suggest a witty and appropriate name, x by y out of z, yes not bad at all. Prince Philip *(Black Booty* by *The Buccaneer* out of *African Queen!)* is the Game's acknowledged master.

But soon his good offices began to lose their power to make the Queen more yielding and more responsive, as the pressure of the virus, now establishing itself in earnest, brought about far-reaching changes in her temperament.

She had missed her chance of eliminating the infection at the earliest stage of its royal progress. The classic procedure at that time would have been to soap and rinse the exposed area, and then to apply a 0.1 per cent solution of cetrimide, or some other quaternary ammonium compound. The Queen, however, had only once had her mouth washed out with soap and water, when she innocently employed an unsuitable expression (which she had heard used by a lady-in-waiting) while at tea with Queen Mary, and Savlon and its equivalents stood no chance of recommending themselves to a palate whose pre-ferred delicacy was a peppermint cream.

So now depression and restlessness became ingrained in her, undermining all her simple pleasures. Normally she had a ready appetite for televised entertainment; straightforward conde-scension seemed refreshing and even admirable after so much sickly homage. It wasn't at all that she became a more demand-ing critic of her chosen viewing (comedy spectacular, play with a plot); but as the tour progressed, willing enjoyment gave way to the sheerest irritability.

Restlessness had taken a more extreme form in the corgi's case; for the day after the encounter in the hall, in effect his last farewell to his mistress, Punchie went missing. The frantic wanderlust typical of canine rabies is an irresistible force, and has been known to induce its victims to cover distances of up to forty miles. According to the most accurate information available, a concentration of only one fox per square mile is

enough to maintain a rabies epizooty; it is to be hoped that
Punchie met with no such density of population in the envi-
rons of Balmoral, or at least made no attempt to pass on his
affliction with a bite. The foxes for their part, and the local
wildlife in general, would have been wise to stay away, if they
wished Punchie's illness to go no further (to be <u>redundant</u>, as
nosologists put it).

The only at all hopeful sign is that rabies in its bat-borne
form tends to be "dumb" or "paralytic" rather than "furious";
so Punchie is unlikely to have travelled far before his collapse.

Although Queen Elizabeth was still some way from the
furious stage, Philip was less and less able as time passed to coax
his wife and sovereign into equanimity. In their first carefree
days in Australia, she was still very much her old amenable self;
once Philip pointed out to her an old photograph of Princess
Anne, wearing a dress unbecomingly short and a pink pompom
hat, which a newspaper had reprinted as part of a gallery of
royal portraits.

He gave a snort of wry amusement. "In our day, dear," he
remarked, "that sort of outfit would only pass muster as après-
rape wear." And the Queen threw back her head to utter her
full-blooded crow of laughter.

But it wasn't long before her disposition was clouded over
by the encroaching illness.

Chief of her prodromal symptoms was a vague feeling of
fever; but the Queen was too much of a trouper to give in to
so feeble a malaise. Nor did she alert her intimates to the
strangeness of the sensations, numbness alternating with pins
and needles, that she was experiencing in the region originally
infected.

Nervous telegrams from anguished outposts piled up in her
Foreign Office; but the threatened bureaucracy was busy elsewhere. Foreign bodies continued their advance, inside the
nerves, towards the headquarters of government.

The inevitable inflammation of nose and mouth was assumed by the Queen's medical advisers to be a recurrence of her sinus trouble, hitherto the only blemish on her good health. They therefore prescribed triturated and succussed potencies of *arsenicum album, atropa belladonna,* and *allium cepa* (white arsenic, deadly nightshade, and onion, to present them in their street clothes), these being the similima recommended for this condition by the canons of homeopathic medicine.

It is at first blush surprising that the Queen should favour even so established a heterodoxy as homeopathy. But the story of her ancestry is also the story of the monarch's transition from owning his country to being its mascot; so what could be more likely to attract the second Elizabeth, than a doctrine which insists that a substance gains overwhelmingly in strength by being crushed and watered down?

During this stage of her illness the Queen's wastepaper-basket marksmanship, normally of a high order and a matter of no small pride to her, suffered a severe decline. If Her Majesty had been in the care of her usual staff, the tell-tale signs, balls of crumpled paper squatting dejected round every monogrammed bin, would not long have gone uninterpreted. As it was, no suspicions were aroused in anyone; even those most officiously concerned with her well-being held only that she was a little strained, emotionally a little under par. Even when whole groups of symptoms began to make themselves felt, denoting progressive central nervous system invasion, the ritually splendid trappings of a royal visit tended to draw attention away from them. So on the occasion of the Sydney civic reception the brilliance of her jewellery, tiara, necklace, earrings, effectively prevented those present at the time from noticing the no less extraordinary appearance of her eyes. Unnaturally wide and staring (muscles affected by impaired cranial nerves), pupils dilated, they show up as splashes of sour

fire in the famous photographs, originally issued to commemo-
rate the festive meal.

Except in this literal sense, the Queen was distinctly lacklus-
tre that evening. Not a conspicuous consumer at the best of
times, she did little justice to the meal, even to her favourite
dish, saddle of lamb; and this although weakened swallowing
muscles are better able to process a solid bolus of food than a
mouthful of liquid. Her moderation in matters of drink (orange
squash always excepted) was so well-known that her effectual
abstinence aroused no comment; it was a matter of record that
a smaller sum was devoted to the Royal Cellars in 1963 than
in 1300.

Certainly no-one supposed that there might be some special
reason for her leaving her glass untouched.

A certain minimum of speculation was excited by her
speech; not of course by its content, but by unexpected quirks
in its delivery. Her Majesty's voice was not by any means under
the usual degree of control; it whooped up to girlish heights at
frequent intervals, and once or twice it failed her completely.

It was almost like the bad old days before Prince Philip
encouraged her to listen to recordings of herself, and helped
her thereby to transform her plummy squeal into a well-
rounded instrument for the projection of her ideals. The small
proportion of the audience which had reservations, on the basis
of this one performance, about Her Majesty's stature as a
public speaker, was all the same very happy to ascribe her
shortcomings to nervousness. It made her seem less remote
somehow.

Prince Philip was sufficiently struck by his wife's change of
voice to observe her closely for a little while, but he had as a
matter of politeness to attend to his nearer neighbours; and he
saw no reason to get unduly worried. He would have needed
supernatural powers to notice the one slight additional sign
from the Queen that all was not well. The indefinite forebod-

ing which is so characteristic a harbinger of the disease's out-
break exaggerated the mildly superstitious side of her personality, which normally took no notice of portents less dire than
broken mirrors and fallen family portraits.

He would have seen her—without breaking off conversation,
admittedly painstaking and far from fluent, with her neighbour
—take a pinch of salt from a little pile spilled on the gleaming
table, and throw it delicately over her left shoulder.

The next morning, her husband and she made sure, in their few
minutes of leisure before starting the day's round of engagements, to observe the first golden rule of royal life (never pass
up an opportunity to take the weight off your feet); the second
commandment (ditto ditto ditto pressure ditto bladder) would
be obeyed nearer the actual time of their departure.

Knowing better than anyone the personal cost to the Queen
of apparently breezy and informal walkabouts like today's,
Philip did his best to chivvy her into cheerfulness. He invited
her to bra sharp her Strine.

"This really is bloody funny I must say," he must have said,
brandishing a paperback. "Come on, I'll teach you how to talk
to the people here. Now then, say We woker meara gain."

"Really Philip."

"Come on. We woker meara gain."

" 'We woker meara gain.' "

"Knotter fiker nairlpit."

" 'Knotter'—oh must I really?"

"No, of course not, not if you don't want to. But listen to
this, this is really brilliant.

With air chew, with air chew,
Iker nardly liver there chew,
An I dreamer badger kisser snite and die.

Phoney wicked beer loan,
Jars-chewer mere nonnair roan,
An weed dreamer batter mooner pinner sky."

"I don't have to say that do I?"
"No but hang on, there's more to come:

With air chew, with air chew,
Hair mike-owner liver there chew?
Wile yerrony immy dream sigh maulwye scrine.
Anna strewer seffner barf
Yuma snow-eye Nietzsche laugh,
Cars with air chew immy arm sit snow-ewe Strine."

"Well now we know how to talk to them I suppose we'd better get a move on," said the Queen, with a real attempt at brightness.

"Righty-ho. But look here, are you all right? I mean you look a shade peaky. . . ."

"I slept badly that's all. I'm fine."

"Poor love. But it's going to be damn hot out there. How about something to drink before we go? Something to cool you down. Or tone you up?"

The Queen declined with little more than the distaste of the self-controlled for any suggestion of indulgence.

"Go on, treat yourself. Just a tiny gin-and-Brownie." Even a joke family must be allowed its family jokes.

"Not even a tiny one." Her Majesty's remark on a 1957 tour that some Brownies cheering and waving flags by the roadside were "a real tonic" had lodged like shrapnel in the Windsor funny-bone.

"Sure you're up to it?" fretted His Royal Highness.

"Quite sure. Mad Dogs and Englishmen," she said with a croak, "Go Out in the Midday Sun."

"Too bloody right. But it's not fair on you."

"Of course it is. It's my job."

"Not much more of it on this trip anyway."

"No, thank the Lord."

"I wasn't a bit popular when I said we weren't here for our health, but really! They haven't the faintest idea. It is absolutely <u>staggering</u> how much they expect us to do. Ready then?"

"Right ready. I'll just pay that call, then we'll be off."

The royal couple started their walkabout together; then they split up, with the Queen dispensing brief hellos to the enthusiastic crowds behind the barriers. A raving queen could not in the normal course of things expect any such welcome from the Australians.

Prince Philip meanwhile had a freer hand, chatting at fair length with individuals or groups that took his fancy. The policeman, plain clothes with a capital P.C., who was doing duty as bodyguard, sauntered anonymously behind them.

The sun flashed down like a ceremonial sword, investing the day with bright heat. It wasn't the weather for walking or talking, but the Queen had her job to do.

"Hello, and how are <u>you</u>?" she ventured at random.

"The better for seeing you, Queen. We're all terrifically loyal here and we all think you're doing a grand job."

"Thank you, thank you." Not only did Her Majesty have gooseflesh; she was sweating uncontrollably. "Isn't it hot though?"

"Cooler than last week, Ma'am."

"Well, it's quite . . . hot enough for me anyway." *I am come amongst you,*

"Your Majesty? When's Charles going to get himself married?"

"We'll . . . let him make up his own mind . . . shall we?"
not for my recreation and sport,

"That's right, Majesty, don't let him be hurried, whatever
you do. All in his own good time."

"Ma'am? Ma'am? Can I kiss you?"

"I'm afraid not . . . it's just . . . one of those things." *but
resolved, in the heat of the battle,*

"Your Majesty, I hope you stay Queen for ever and ever. We
love you."

"You're . . . very kind, most kind. And where are you from?"
to live or die amongst you;

"I live in Sydney, Ma'am, but I was born in Leeds, Ma'am."

"How interesting." *to lay down my crown and my blood,*

"Your Majesty, I saw you here in Sydney in 1954."

"I'm so glad. I hope . . . I hope you see me many more
times." *even in the dust,*

"I hope so too, Your Majesty, I really do."

"Is this your little boy?" *for my God and my people.*

"No, Your Majesty. I don't know who he belongs to."

The unclaimed child was meanwhile slipping through the
barrier, and issued from between a pair of policemen to con-
front his sovereign. He smiled and thrust towards her a tiny
plastic corgi, once part of a keyring. The Queen stooped with
difficulty to receive it. As an offering, this was well in the
Widow's Mite class; it was no small thing for the boy to part
with almost a lifelong resident of his mouth. The spectators
could now see the tears running freely down Her Majesty's
face; they blamed a full heart (rather than rogue ducts flaring
up one final time) for the exaggerated lacrimation.

"Thank you . . . very much. What's . . . your name, sweet-
heart?" *I know that I have but the body*

The child gave a merry little laugh, said nothing.

"You there, hello . . . are you . . . this little boy's mother?"
of a weak and feeble woman,

The girl addressed by the Queen, standing in the crowd with her very best girlfriend, was too nervous and overcome to reply; the pair of them looked at each other for a moment, then turned bright red and exploded with hysterical laughter.

"Well, you . . . must belong . . . to somebody . . . mustn't you . . . pet?" *but I have the heart of a King,* "I'm sure . . . your mother . . ." *and of a King of England.*

But she was already forgetting the little boy, gift, missing mother, and all. She took a few unsteady steps; then, pulling herself together, she squared her shoulders, and raised her eyes towards a fresh section of the crowd.

In the centre of her field of vision a cup of white plastic asserted itself.

The tense surface of the dark-brown fluid was agitated by rising shapes; gassy globes, ellipsoids.

The liquid had been there for ever, independent of the ribbed vessel which held it in, and of the tanned fist which held it up.

A web of bubbles shimmered at its lip.

On its rippled and fizzing skin the sun balanced an intolerable anagram.

The relentless cordial flirted with the Queen's long-suppressed thirst, drenching her heart with terror of its glistening waters.

This is the intriguing associative mechanism of hydrophobia. The Queen's resident virus had dined long and well on the inhibitory circuits which would normally damp down and regulate her protective reflexes of coughing and sneezing. These reflexes were now liable to function in an exaggerated form on the slightest pretext; or even of their own accord. The classic pretext is of course the act of drinking; debilitated pharyngeal muscles are only too likely to admit liquid to the larynx entrance and the back of the nose, triggering muscle spasm and panic.

This very morning the patient found she had to force herself to do her toothbrush duty; and a rinse was somehow out of the question, so she went to face the world with faint traces of a minty froth on her lips.

More oblique stimuli for the head-jerking, arm-tossing, and back-bending of the hydrophobic seizure are draughts of air in the face, water on the skin, attempts to speak, loud noises, bright lights; the sight, sound, or mention of water.

In this context "water" clearly includes cola; so the pressure on the Queen's constitution to give in to the racking spasm of opisthotonic convulsion could hardly have been more total. That she was able in any measure to resist says much for her hard-won ability to blot out events of the most eclipsing urgency. She staggered, but it was a stagger worthy of a queen; and she was able to swing her slipping and unwieldy eyes into a passable focus, as she faced her audience once more.

Impossible at this stage of the circuitry's dissolution definitively to establish causes for what happened next.

Resistance to the hydrophobic frenzy may have been a thing of a few moments only, deferring the throes but not precluding them. Her adversary could not forever be warded off; had she not fought hard, fought well, our Lady of Windsor? Or the appearance before her, multiplied by her dying eyes but otherwise quite clear, of a hat perched on the nearest matronly curls, may very well have prompted the cataclysm.

Down to the last flourish of desiccated coconut, it was modelled on a ten-year-old mode of Her Majesty's; and her sight of it may have been the crucial factor which made her stop dead in the way that she did. Her mouth hanging open, she stared rigidly at the unforgivable millinery.

She had always favoured a killing stare as the best means of silencing an individual or annihilating a remark; but on this occasion she could do nothing to abbreviate her glare, or to soften its antagonism.

The convention that any exchange of words must be inaugurated by Royalty may have contributed to the deadlock; though it was less powerful a force than it had been in the past. Queen Victoria once rebuked a maid for drawing her attention to a small fire, caused by a stray coal, in progress on her outskirts.

Silence communicated itself to the crowd, tense with the expectation of an unspeakable breach. An alien force, from beyond the bounds of space and time, in no way subject to their laws, was invading the fragile continuum of etiquette.

The face below the hat lost the stunned brightness of its first smile; the eyes in the grip of the Queen's evil astigmatism trembled with uncertainty. Where was the bland little personage of the previous decades, butt of so much criticism, unadventurous and banal? Where was the petite conformist whose strongest feelings were a dislike of ivy, a prejudice against magenta?

Somewhere on the fogged plate of the Queen's mind an image, long stored away, of public freedom and a shared abandonment, was beginning to glow. V-E Night, and a unique sally into the streets of a crowded London; Lilibet and Margo slipping into the cheering mobs with only a pair of young officers for escorts, Lil and Margo linking arms with strangers, calling with the rest for King and Queen to come out onto the balcony for their accolade. Lilibet in mounting ecstasy knocking hats off heads too light or tight to care while—did she notice?—the escorts mounted guard on her own demure little number.

She was free, she was herself, and she was real. Never before had she been so uninhibited.

Sharp-eyed Philip was turning, was making his swift way towards her. The bodyguard, cursing himself in sudden fear that he had been over-discreet and under-watchful, began to pound heavily after him. The straining crowd, collectively sure it was missing something, at last burst its banks and surged forward.

The Queen's kid gloves were still in place, though lightly soiled after even so short an exposure to the populace, as she raised her arm, as if executing the first stages of a leisurely salute, then stabbed out convulsively, so as to land a divine right on the guilty headgear; which went flying, fur fabric and frill, just as the crowd converged on the subsiding figure of its monarch.

It was no longer V-E Night, it was no longer even Europe; but it was a great victory for all that.

My first duty to the reader is perhaps to explain how I came to be in charge of what, in another clime, and in circumstances of malfeasance rather than misfortune, would undoubtedly be termed a "cover-up."

The Queen's departure from Australia being suddenly advanced as a result of her unwell condition, there travelled with her on the small aeroplane supplied at short notice for her convenience by the great courtesy of the Australian Government only her physician, her Private Secretary, her Press Secretary, her equerry, two ladies-in-waiting, two dressers, and a detective. The rest of us in the royal party—her hairdresser, her six footmen, two maids, four clerks, and myself, her Associate Private Secretary—were to travel home on board *Britannia* as originally planned, after Prince Philip had, at Her Majesty's express and very characteristic request, fulfilled her remaining engagements.

When precise news of the Queen's state reached him, the Prince had only a single further appointment on his schedule, namely the centenary celebrations of the Grand Order of Swagmen; but he nevertheless declined to cancel it. In his private capacity as the Queen's consort, he might long more than anything to be at her side with all speed, but as her representative he must discharge to the full the duty laid upon him by his monarch, whatever the agony it might cost. Prince Philip and his staff therefore left Australia a full two days after the Queen; but not before he had entrusted me personally with the task of preventing news of the tragedy now gripping the royal house, and of course the disease itself, from spreading any further. To this end he had secured the co-operation of the Australian police and guaranteed me the authority to implement any decisions I might make in the course of my endeavours.

No knowledge of the ways of protocol is needed to appreciate that, whatever her legal position might prove to be, for the Head of the Commonwealth to pass on hydrophobia even to one of her subjects would be enough to overturn at a stroke the public relations campaigns of a generation. This is particularly true of the present case, inasmuch as the Australian authorities have spared no pains to maintain the freedom from the disease enjoyed by their country since 1867.

The bodyguard who had accompanied the Queen on the crucial "walkabout" had been at too discreet a distance throughout the incident to be of much help as a witness; but a hurried scrutiny of the rabies literature convinced me that even without hard evidence of a potentially hazardous encounter, and despite the melancholy truth that no treatment may be relied upon, swift medical action was called for. Given that an infected rabbit was, on one occasion in Alberta, Canada, observed to advance on a dog and bite it severely, might not the virus overcome even Her Majesty's shyness and cause her to lash out? On the credit side was the fact that almost half of those bitten by a known subject do not in fact develop the disease, but this good news was more than offset by the information that an actual bite is not necessary for transmission of the infection, the virus in the sufferer's saliva being perfectly well able to penetrate intact mucous membrane, or to enter the body through even a minor break in the skin.

Press coverage of Her Majesty's indisposition and return to England hinted at nothing untoward, nor was there any communication direct from the public on the subject; but the possibility that the Queen had afflicted one or more of her interlocutors could not on that account be disregarded, since those who find themselves informally face to face with their sovereign are in a state of shock to start with, and in no condition to register the details of the encounter. An infinitely more likely possibility than that of a bite as such, though, was that a member of the crowd had taken advantage of the Queen's undeniably disordered state in order to snatch a royal kiss, or to press upon her some vulnerable baby for inspection and approval. I felt it would be foolish to underestimate the desire on the part of the public to grapple as closely as possible with the person of its monarch; and the possible outcome in this particular case of that universal desire.

So it was that the day after receiving the terrible news from England I had not only a medical team well stocked with the relevant serums and antidotes and prepared for the business ahead, but also a plan of campaign ready to be put into action. By this time the resolution was clear in my mind that those who had come into close contact with the Queen during the brief period of her loss of control in the streets of Sydney should receive the most thorough medical help that it lay within my power to provide; but there were two equally clear obstacles to any direct approach to those people, perhaps numbering twenty in all, who had been at risk. One was that undisguised medical attention would be sure to reveal that unparalleled constitutional and personal crisis which it was part of my brief to keep a secret from the public and from the Press; while the other, perhaps more important, was that the course of treatment designed to deter rabies from establishing itself, consisting as it must if it is to achieve its maximum effectiveness of a massive injection of anti-serum in the stomach, succeeded by a further administration of vaccine every day for a fortnight, is considerably more unpleasant and more painful than are most diseases, and would certainly be undersubscribed in the absence of an element of indirection.

Accordingly I resorted, in my efforts to round up possible victims, to no crude revelation that the personage glimpsed by her loyal subjects in the streets had been, in effect, mad and extremely dangerous, but instead issued a non-committal statement, which was run in all the newspapers and was moreover prominently featured both by radio and the television, to the effect that those members of the public who had met Queen Elizabeth the Second on her recent "walkabout" in Sydney were invited to present themselves at Government House at any time after nine o'clock the next morning. I spent the rest of the day organising the details of the forthcoming Operation Pinprick and retired early, passing the night in one of a suite of rooms commandeered in Government House and in part adapted to some new functions, on a camp bed rigged up there for my benefit.

I was not much surprised to be awoken by a vague tumult the next morning, some considerable time before the hour set by my communiqué; I had in fact taken the precaution of arranging for the police to be on duty in large numbers from six o'clock onwards. Just before nine an officer slipped in to inform me that those waiting numbered about seven hundred; this too was hardly unexpected. I was ready for them.

At nine o'clock prompt the first hundred or so of the postulants were ushered in by a small handful of policemen; their colleagues had instructions the meanwhile to discourage anyone from leaving the queue, by muttering in a rueful tone of voice that some people had all the luck, whenever they felt that this announcement would have the desired effect.

I had even readied myself for the more extreme of the clichés which were presented to me by this first of many groups, once my eyes had adjusted sufficiently to the brightness of its costume for me to see it with any distinctness: the infants in arms, the man already confined to a wheelchair, and the eighty-three-year-old phenomenon who boasted that she had crocheted bootees for the Queen's toddlerhood, and had rendered the same service to each little Prince and Princess in turn.

I hoped, and was most probably justified in so doing, that my face conveyed to my audience an impression of authoritative blandness as I allowed the hubbub to die down at its own pace before I started to speak. When I did so, it was, at least at first, with a carefully rehearsed lack of engagement or emphasis. On the other side of the wall behind me were waiting hundreds of capacious syringes, thousands of stout and sterilised needles, and gallons on gallons of health-giving gamma-globulin, all primed and prepared by a hand-picked medical team.

"Fellow citizens of the Commonwealth," I began. "Australia is a large place; a vast country of great contrasts and unimaginable distances." I realised well enough that an announcement of this sort did little to justify the rallying-call I had disseminated by way of the media, but my rhetoric needed a little time to get properly under way. "But, large as it is, Australia has no monopoly on the time and the attention of our Sovereign Lady the Queen. It is her duty and her privilege to travel the entire globe, keeping the image of that continuity and that order which she so signally represents constantly before the eyes of all nations; she makes her namesake the first Elizabeth, who never ventured beyond her frontiers, seem a feeble stay-at-home by contrast with her untiring efforts. What part of the world has she neglected to visit in her travels of the past quarter of a century? Every year of her reign has seen fresh exertions and fresh triumphs, fresh barriers between ruler and ruled, between man and man, decisively overthrown.

"More than twenty years ago, when Her Majesty was very much in the prime of her young womanhood, the fear was expressed, in no less exalted a quarter than the columns of the medical journal *The Lancet,* that she was taxing herself over-much by undertaking such consistently onerous tours of duty. Throughout her career, the Queen has paid the price, and paid it to the full; that none but her intimates should have any inkling of the penalties attendant on so keen a sense of duty has always been her dearest wish. Now, alas, the whole world has learned at last how recklessly she has squandered her re-sources in the interests of that tired abstraction, the brother-hood of man, which she, surely, has done more than anyone else living to render a real and accomplished fact."

Such quantities of well-marshalled semi-relevance could be relied upon to have an effect approaching that of hypnosis on my antipodean listeners. Then I judged that it was time for me to shift my ground.

"And yet. And yet. Big as the world is, prodigious as are the distances the Queen has travelled—reputably estimated as the equivalent of sixteen times the earth's circumference—she has not spread herself so thin as to be forgetful of any single one of those who love her. One would have to be jaded indeed not to treasure the memory of loyalty in its purest and most electric essence. If you have given thought to the matter, you will no doubt have concluded that Her Majesty has already long since forgotten you and your city, that she has taken away with her nothing more than a blurred impression of familiar actions and predictable encounters. After all, what country, what city, what community does not excel itself and break all bounds in its eagerness to welcome the Queen with its most overwhelming display? How could Sydney hope for more than an insignificant place in her sovereign's affections?

"And yet you would be wrong to think these things. Eliza-beth your Queen retains an image as sharp and lasting as diamond of your city, and more particularly of those of her subjects whom she has been privileged to meet at close quarters and without formality, yes, of you. And—you may laugh, you may find it absurd, but it is true—she feels she has let you down."

One or two of them did, amazingly enough, utter little derisive laughs, did apparently find it absurd. I had of course stationed a few policemen in plain clothes in the ranks of the crowd, ready to give the mass emotions any cue they might need, but nothing of the sort was in fact called for. My audience was already choking with gratified loyalty and love.

"The Queen feels she must make up to you for her inability to accomplish in full the tasks she has set herself; even in her exhausted condition, with her physicians urging her in the strongest possible terms to spare herself, to rest, she insisted on making her wishes known to me. She is most anxious that you all be rewarded for the exemplary devotion you have shown her, and that you receive some consolation for that early departure from your shores which she so sincerely regrets."

The Australian people is I suppose an open-hearted one, unused to displays of kindness from strangers, easily moved by the emotions of others; by this time, at any rate, most of my listeners were quaking with sincerity and were loudly singing "For She's a Jolly Good Fellow," and even "Here's a Health unto Her Majesty."

"The Queen's idea," I continued, "and I think you will agree with me that it is one of her happiest inspirations, is that now she is unable to complete her visit to your country, you must come and see her. This is not to say, I'm afraid, that she will be able to see you personally, for after all, her engagement books were filled up a good long time ago—and in any case she must devote herself to building up her strength before anything else. But she has authorised me to arrange on your behalf, and without your being expected to contribute even a penny towards the cost, a fortnight's holiday of the most unsparing luxury in London, seat of Her Majesty's Government and not least among the jewels of her crown. Sixty thousand devotees made the costly and exhausting journey from Australia for the sake of attending her Coronation all those years ago, one lady from Brisbane even selling her house in order to do so; in this age of a comparable if not a greater austerity, she hopes you will do her honour by accepting her small gesture of love acknowledged and returned."

It hardly needs to be said that by now the applause was tumultuous and general. I sat down, and waited for silence gradually to re-establish itself before I spoke again, this time in the tone of someone who desires to settle trivial details without waste of time. "The date of your departures has been provisionally set for a fortnight on Monday, to give you time to make your own preparations; if this doesn't suit, you must inform my staff and they'll do their very best to accommodate you. And now if you'll line up, in alphabetical order if you please, we'll see about getting you kitted up with the documents and so on that you'll be needing."

In a matter of moments Adams, Keith J., was being affably escorted into the next room, where he filled in some meaningless forms, date of birth 4 April 1903, marital status single, before being conducted to one of the impromptu operating theatres for a jab. He was told it was an anti-tetanus booster, which he would need for his forthcoming travels, and he then received a large intramuscular injection of human anti-rabies gamma-globulin. An airline ticket for the London–Sydney part of the journey was pressed into his hand. Finally he was several times instructed to come back next day, for the rest of the papers he would need for the holiday of his lifetime.

I spent only a few moments making sure that all the machinery was working as it should; then I presented myself to my next audience, awaiting me in another room down the corridor.

Sometimes I laid it on more thickly (the reader is entirely at liberty not to believe me), sometimes I was more sparing of the pomp and circumstance; but I had no great difficulty in carrying my auditors with me.

A certain sophistication of method notwithstanding, my device did not differ in any important respect from that of the doctor who gives a freshly inoculated child a sweet for having been a good boy; my problem over the next fortnight being the location, or if need be the invention, of sweets sufficiently consoling to appease the suffering travellers-to-be and to ensure that they reappeared the next day, if only to safeguard the boons already received.

The consolation gifts, though, demanded the most careful assessment; they must be to the required degree attractive, but not so wonderful as to arouse the suspicions of the recipients. However likely it was that the Australians in my care would go through fire if, say, membership of the Order of the Garter were in prospect (supposing for a moment that it lay within my power to make that award), they would presumably inspect such an offer for signs of an ulterior motive. A secondary problem for me that fortnight was the devising of a fresh disease each day, to account for the continuing ravages wrought by the inoculating teams.

In order to anticipate the objections which were to be expected from my Australians when it dawned on them that the vaccinations showed every sign of going on forever, I briefed my staff to be ready with rebuttals of every sort. Someone, for instance, might ask what today's injection was for, and on hearing it was to guard against diphtheria, might insist, with his or her voice regaining something of its former brashness, that he or she had for certain sure already had that shot. In such a case the reply was to be *"not Asian diphtheria you haven't,"* or something along similar lines. The insistence on the belly rather than the arm or buttock as the site of the debilitating injections could be attributed to the notorious rigour of EEC regulations. More generalised resentments, and

signs of a growing hankering after a life of unperforated dull-
ness in Sydney in preference to the charms of London bought
dear, were to be combated with some such tactic as a compari-
son between the actual low threshold of pain observed among
the Australian subjects, and the tough image (bush-rangers,
Ned Kelly, Bill the Bullocky) enjoyed by their countrymen
abroad.

Day Two (cholera) got us off to a good start with the presentation to each person inoculated of a set of keys for a multiple-
starred hotel room in London. A Harrods voucher to the value
of twenty pounds, not genuine in any strict sense but sure to
be honoured once I had pulled the right strings, seemed a
happy thought for Day Three (anthrax). Government presses
turned out a very plausible Red Rover Bus Pass to sugar the pill
on Day Four (smallpox), while a deluxe camera and film set did
something to kiss it better on Day Five (undulant fever).

Thereafter I confess my inspiration failed me. Things went
decidedly downhill when I distributed block bookings and bar
vouchers for the National Theatre (diphtheria), and followed
that with altogether bogus Goldentourist Special Passes for
Scotland Yard (tularemia), the Post Office Tower (typhoid),
the Houses of Parliament (St. Louis encephalitis), Broadcast-
ing House (whooping-cough), Printing House Square (polio)
and Westminster Abbey (equine encephalomyelitis).

I was beginning to feel once again that I had run dry, that
I had exhausted the capital's supply of splendours and ameni-
ties, when luckily the rot was stopped to some extent by the
discovery of two treasure-troves in Government House itself:
firstly, a cache of framed photographs of Winston Churchill,
one of them (and eventually all of them) even signed; and
secondly, a huge slab of Prince Edward's christening cake,
covered with monograms and baroque green icing. This last
must have derived from the Commonwealth tradition of bak-
ing dozens of the things to welcome royal infants into the

world, though no-one knew how it had come to take up residence in a Government House deep-freeze, presumably at some time in 1964. It proved to be a little dank, but otherwise quite good. In this way my patients were tempted through Day Thirteen (yellow fever) and Day Fourteen (Japanese B encephalitis), even if few were in cake-eating mood.

The other half of the air tickets, the Sydney-to-London portion, was at last surrendered on Day Fifteen. No-one could have been more relieved and pleased than I was; it is idle to pretend that the stress of the whole operation had had no effect on me. Rocky Mountain spotted fever. I blessed its name.

B O O K

T H R E E

The Queen moves smoothly through a hushed, blank corridor; purple airspace as it's called, cleared of competing traffic for five miles on each side in the interests of this so special passenger.

She is in good hands. Prudence Faber likes nothing better than to give her friend and mistress just a little bit of mothering. At the best of times the Queen needs extra care when a tour comes to its end; she is always thin and strained after so much concentrated effort. But this time Prudence can't help feeling that Her Majesty isn't quite trying her hardest, isn't really keeping her end up as she should.

She shows no interest in the tempting historical novels Prudence has looked out for her; even her juiciest ancestors, doomed, tragic, or just plain bad, have no charm for her in her present mood. A half-completed crossword puzzle from the Daily Telegraph (tricky but just this side of diabolical) is to hand, but the Queen shows no trace of her normal desire to polish it off. For once she is immune to her most tried and tested pastimes.

Prudence asks her mistress if perhaps she is unhappy with the slightly ramshackle nature of the present arrangements—the regular Queen's flight is of course more thoroughly adapted for the convenience and comfort of the globe-trotting monarch. She gets no answer from the preoccupied Queen.

In her capacity as Her Majesty's "good right hand" Prudence is perfectly familiar with the Queen's foibles. After prolonged subjection to public scrutiny, or at moments of stress, she has funny spells which produce just this sort of unresponsive trance. It's as if she only knows who she is when she's on show.

Prudence prepares to break the spell in the usual way, with a wand of barley-sugar, sovereign alike against nerves and travel-sickness. After all, air travel has never appealed very much to the Queen. On her grandfather's orders she has been carried across the lawns to meet Lindbergh in triumph, and on her own initiative she has entertained Major Yuri Gagarin; but she likes to have solid ground or soaring horseflesh underneath her, and she more often dreams of fall than flight.

Prudence peels back the cellophane on a sample stick from her stockpile and passes it across.

After a further long moment of silence, the Queen takes Prudence's offering and pokes it between her lips. She runs her dry tongue over it a few slow times, then manages with some effort to speak. "I feel rather poorly, you know, Prudence," she says.

"Of course you do," staunchly declares Prudence. "It's hardly surprising. I keep saying you let them push you too hard, but you can't bear letting anyone down. Never mind, dear; perhaps the doctor will give you something to make you sleep."

"That would be nice," enunciates the Queen. And she

shows her enthusiasm by crunching the pills up, when they come, without benefit of water, for all the world as if she is one of her corgi darlings demolishing the day's ration of biscuits.

Soon she is unconscious; and Prudence has only herself to look after. For forty minutes she wrestles with the Telegraph crossword, sucking furiously for inspiration on the discarded barley-sugar, without solving even a single clue.

DR. BULL: It didn't actually matter how much or how little the Princess said or did, what feelings she might try to pour into her words and her actions; she was a fact rather than a person, and as such was both overwhelming and utterly flat. She was such a source of amazement that she could never hope to be a surprise. So why did she bother trying to shine, when the vaguest approximation to competence would in any case be represented as supreme accomplishment, just as boredom and nerves have throughout her career emerged in print as poise and animation? There was for instance the story, very popular at the time, that the Princess triumphantly crowned her time with the A.T.S. at Camberley by driving a heavy truck up to London during the blackout and into the courtyard of the Palace; subtract inventions like the heaviness of the truck (in fact a staff car) and the nocturnal setting, and you are left with nothing so very remarkable—which is of course why those details were added. In the interests of the image, incongruous details could be suppressed just as easily as impressive ones could be manufactured; and so the newspapers made no mention of the less than glamorous fact that No. 230873 Second Subaltern Elizabeth Windsor, No. 1 Mechanical Transport Training Centre, returned to the Castle each evening for her dinner, her bed, and her breakfast.

I have said enough already to make it plausible that the young Elizabeth should have inevitably building up in her, as a counterweight to that "reasonableness" which should perhaps have worried rather than reassured her guardians, a longing for real company, for a mutually guaranteed reality, that dwarfed mere love in the intensity of its need.

It is worth mentioning at this point that Royal Family life can never be an inspirational example to the People, simply because it is a defensive alliance against the People's oppressive interest and attention. If for instance my wife was embarking on a six-month, fifty-thousand-mile tour of the world, involving thirteen thousand handshakes and the delivery of 157 speeches, I would certainly not expect to be cooked breakfast by her on the morning of her departure. I might well accompany her, perhaps walk alongside her with my hands clasped behind my back, even bark and glare at intrusive lights, cameras, journalists. But in doing so I would hardly be furnishing my subjects with an ideal of family life for them to base their mortgaged microcosms on.

At the time of her growing friendship with Philip, her father was concerned by the fact that his Lilibet had apparently fallen for the first eligible bachelor she had come across; but he needn't have worried. By this I don't mean that Philip was destined from the dawn of time to restore Lilibet's Platonic wholeness—though of course he had advantages, quite apart from that height and that fair colouring which had always been the Princess' ideal; as a member of the Royal Family of Greece, he was her equal, but he had a down-to-earthness which must have struck Lilibet as quite staggeringly real—did not the house in Corfu where he was born bear the name of *Mon Repos*? I mean rather, that anyone not disqualified by the grossest of defects would do a woman in her position as much good as any foreordained soul-mate; seen in this light, the fact that her sister Margaret has contrived such prodigies of discord in her private life says much for her energy and her desire to be different.

Philip's adjustment to his new role, always a fascinating subject of study, particularly repays attention in the first few years after his wife's accession; it is during this period that he starts to diverge markedly from the image fostered by the pre-wedding propaganda, that of the quintessential Englishman enjoying a relationship of easy mutual respect with the gentlemen of the Press, and to develop his ersatz abrasiveness of personality.

The impression of a life of anachronistic leisure for the lucky consort which royal nuptials give could not be more illusory, as a glance at the small print of the marriage contract will speedily tell us. The nominal supreme stallion of the royal stud in fact ends up as a gelding; the Queen Bee's spouse has no option but to share her status as drone.

At first it seemed that Philip was making a breakthrough; unlike his wife, he learned fairly readily that conscientiousness was no part of his role. On at least one ceremonial drive at Royal Ascot he gave most of his attention to a cricket commentary on his pocket radio; and after the minimum time on show in the royal box retired to an inner room equipped with a television, in order to follow the game in earnest.

But Philip's breezy attitude to the world is less real than apparent because his new position changes everything, not only imposing on him an arduous round of empty duties, but also depriving his genuine interests of their substance; rendering them no less artificial than any other rich man's hobbies. Many of his pronouncements, some of them the cause of controversy, others less noticed by the world at large, deal directly with this unique plight of his. Few, for example, would contest his claim to be "one of the most governed people you could expect to meet," or would disagree with his suggestion that the Prisoners' Aid Society might do worse than to succour the Windsors. Another of his remarks, to the effect that "we live in the most regimented society ever in this country," less defensibly applies his observations to the nation as a whole, but perhaps we can detect here a half-suppressed desire rather than a straightforward comment—it would be surprising if such a prisoner, baffled and unable to free himself, did not at some level wish his fate of incarceration on others.

Philip's declared approbation of the virtues of conscription should also be taken in this spirit, and not be dismissed, as it has been in the past, as a piece of impertinent Balmoral Rearmament ballyhoo. But his presumably genuine impatience with formal occasions and formal clothes, with "pomping up" as he calls it, intermittently deceives the Prince into thinking that there is a part for him to play, as an independent and free-wheeling critic, in the moral life of the realm. There is not. The Windsor mavericks are as unreal as the pseudo-martyrs they are so concerned not to resemble. However often he decides to stir things up a bit, by referring to a Henry Moore bronze as a "monkey's gallstone," or by diagnosing a further strain of the English disease, Philip can never be offbeat any more than a metronome can; and his discarding of convention is as illusory as his wife's embracing of it. He can't be both an icon and an iconoclast; it isn't safe. Philip has failed to follow up in his life the consequences of his statement that "I know as well, if not better than anyone here, that life in Britain is not wholly rational."

All the information which the princely antennae pick up is bogus; yet Philip does his best to abide by it. A fair representative of the meaningless quality of the messages received by royalty would be the clock at the Queen's Birthday Parade, the ritual of Trooping the Colour, which is advanced or retarded as needed in order to strike eleven just as the Queen enters the parade-ground, on a horse so thoroughly exercised (to prevent excessive friskiness) as barely to be conscious. The monarch must always be seen to be on time; but if she wanted to know what the time actually was, would anybody tell her?

Philip once outlined his conception of his job: "I try to react to what I suppose people expect," he said, which could hardly be a more classic capitulation to the unreal. How are you to react, when you only ever see people who are already reacting to you? The world tempts you towards full-time play-acting with its most bewitching displays of cardboard.

The obvious model of personality to use here is that which distinguishes between "gyroscopes" and "radar-watchers." A "gyroscope" is someone who leads his life in accordance with his own ideas, and has no need of the respect or notice of others in order to carry on. A "radar-watcher" by contrast seeks always to be guided by the blips of other people's reactions to him, and defines himself solely in other people's terms. It goes without saying that these caricatures represent the extremes of a continuum; a perfect gyroscope would be a solipsist and egomaniac, just as an absolute radar-watcher would end up, baffled by contradictory blips, as a schizophrenic chameleon. In their different ways Elizabeth and Philip have come dangerously close to this extreme of radar-watching.

Princess Elizabeth's own chameleon, brought home for her by Earl Mountbatten when on leave, soon went into a decline; no resourcefulness of pigment could make tolerable an enforced alternation between *The Blue Fairy Book* and *Debrett*.

Even before the death of George VI the royal couple had been given ample evidence of the folly of acting in good faith towards the Absurd. Duke and Princess touched down early in February 1952 at Nairobi, and made a point of deferring any personal plans in order to visit a hospital within an hour of their arrival. The maternity hospital in question was brand-new, had been chosen for that reason so as to make a good impression on the visitors, and, four hours earlier, had housed not a single patient. A matching set of suitable mothers and babies was accordingly rounded up from other institutions; every bed was filled and the desired effect produced. Mirror was duly held up to mirror (both of them distorting, naturally), and everyone was satisfied; the difference between the participants being that for the Africans, their charade was a treat in itself, while for the royal party it was only part of a long-term and unconscious imposture which involved all the tedium of a constant character, without any of the beneficial self-sufficiency of a whole personality.

We should hardly be surprised that a mind which tries to respond to such deranged stimuli ends up by asserting that Kenya's system of plumbing is superior to Ireland's, after spending just six nights in the presidential suite of the New Stanley Hotel in Nairobi.

Many other incidents in recent royal history are reminiscent of the maternity-hospital story; the inhabitants of Lagos, for instance, having heard that headgear should be removed in the presence of royalty, bought hats in their hundreds and thousands for the 1956 royal visit, so as to oblige by taking them off. So perhaps the Queen thinks Nigerians are naturally fond of hats.

It is ironic in the circumstances that dressing up, charades, and play-acting of all sorts should be such favourite pastimes of the royals, that a brief change of part, such as dressing up as maid and waiter for an American Ambassador's fancy-dress ball, should bring so much relief to lifelong performers.

But do they realise they are acting? Marie-Antoinette liked nothing better at Versailles than to dress up in rustic clothes with ladies of her inmost circle, and play at being milkmaids in the mock farms and villas round the Petit Trianon; but artificiality is no longer available in small enough doses for it to continue being a pleasure. In our times the tendency of bad self-consciousness to drive out good has reached an extraordinary pitch; so that the mock farms of the Windsors are run on the most modern and progressive lines. The record milk-yield of Royal Zobo becomes the subject of excited tea-time conversation; no effort is spared to make it look as though the role of farmer is the authentic, rugged, countryman's face, below all masks.

Refusal to question your own solidity doesn't, alas, save you from quantities of fibbing and make-believe; though it would be uncharitable to take the Queen to task for stretching the truth once in a way, as she did, say, when she shared one of her domestic secrets with miners' wives in Sheffeville, Canada, on a tour of their prefab homes. "I find it difficult keeping my floors clean, too," she murmured, which in view of her two-hundred-man staff and Household of four hundred, comes close to the upper limit of size for a little white lie.

When royalty plays at being real in public, it is all too often given away by the sheer scale of the stage-management. When for the purpose of sweetening public relations Prince Charles attended Aberystwyth University in 1969 for a nine-week crash course in Welsh, the Palace insisted he be treated just like any other student; and he was accordingly allotted a room of the usual dimensions. The double-sized warden's flat which had been reserved for him by the University went to a member of his detective entourage instead.

But these unconscious charades are unfortunately carried over into private life. A case can be made out for occasionally presenting a facade even to employees and servants; perhaps it was a justifiable stratagem after the Queen's twenty-eighth birthday celebrations, held on board the *Gothic* en route for Aden, to slip the remains of the cake overboard in a furtive ceremony of burial at sea (a party hat serving as winding-sheet), so as to spare the patissier's feelings. Moreover, many of the private pantomimes of royalty are quite consciously undertaken, healthy and jolly games designed to keep everybody cheerful.

So the royal train on a gruelling tour of Canada was the scene of many colourful japes: imitation bread rolls squealed when touched, fake bell-pushes administered mild electric shocks, joke snakes lay in wait in boxes of "Mixed Nuts," and Philip even chased the shrieking Lilibet from compartment to compartment wearing an enormous set of vampire fangs. And Elizabeth in her turn had a chance to lighten the atmosphere when the couple were reunited at Montijo airport in 1957, amid persistent rumours of a "royal rift." Having heard of a beard-growing contest on board Philip's ship, the Queen rigged up her ladies-in-waiting and herself with postiche face-fungus and embraced her husband with joyful cries of "mind my beard!"

But once an unacknowledged artificiality has established itself, it tends to subvert everything in sight; so that in private as well as in public the Windsors neither tell the truth nor relish the fiction. For how else are we to interpret the gala highlight of the celebrations preceding the Princess Alexandra–Angus Ogilvy nuptials in 1963—so overwhelming as to prompt from the Queen a croon of "we've never had such a day!"—when Philip hired a couple of coaches to take sixty-odd European royals on a mystery tour featuring a pub lunch in the King's Head at Bray?

F O U R

England, and St. George in silver effigy, fixed complete with dragon onto the bright bonnet of a Daimler Straight-Eight, maroon with a fine red stripe, fresh from Royal Mews.

It is Prudence's clear priority to convey the Queen, in all safe haste, to Buckingham Palace; there to embark on the serious business of regaining her most perfect health, in surroundings both rural and urban, central and congenial. She settles her drowsy mistress in the car, arranging a rug in a tartan designed by Victoria round her knees, then takes her own place, poised to make herself useful the moment an occasion arises.

In the front compartment, beyond a panel of smoked glass, the detective asks the driver if he may light a cigarette. Prudence cannot hear them speak, but has no need just now of the intercom in order to communicate; she catches the driver's eye and smiles her readiness to proceed on the journey.

London's night-time streets are not at their most welcoming, nor their most dry. Gleaming wipers usher rivulets of dirty water from the slick frontage of the windscreen. Unheard, their regular movements still capture much of Prudence's attention; she is exhausted, unable to concentrate on more important matters. In her prime she would be ashamed to let a mere tour take it out of her like this. Nothing is as simple as it used to be. Wearing herself out is the only thing that seems to get easier.

In the light of a patrician dashboard, boosted by a Woodbine's dim glow, detective and driver are making conversation of a slack, indifferent kind; the driver is used to keeping his mind as blank as his present number-plate, and gives mechanical answers to questions which are themselves the product of professional habit rather than urgency. A compatible enough pair, robot and sponge, helping each other to stay awake and within reason alert, as they carry Majesty on its weary way home.

Prudence finds herself slipping off to sleep; to her blurring senses the vast interior of the car comes to resemble some grouse-moor of thick-tufted carpet. The opaque screen which separates her from the driver's compartment becomes her horizon, the dim extreme of her perceptions.

Abruptly, Prudence realises that if she doesn't pull herself together and clear her head, she will be of little use to her Queen. Shaking herself, she presses the button which causes the windows smugly to subside, and holds it down for a few seconds. The cold air she has summoned slides in through the opening to refresh her; but turns out to have a stronger animating influence on her employer.

Its chilly impact on the Queen's cheek arouses her to consciousness, and to a characteristically frantic little seizure.

She lurches almost to her feet, lashing out at no enemy in particular. Prudence's only wish has been ever to serve her ruler with all her loyal and well-ordered soul; so it is unjust that she should be knocked insensible by the Queen's random pokes and spasms. The royal handbag, a Harrods item of quite extraordinary stoutness (its corners specially reinforced), makes decisive contact, during its flailings at the end of a convulsed arm, with Prudence's forehead, on whose crumpled surface an expression of devoted concern and bafflement is just beginning to appear. Prudence collapses back into the yielding upholstery as her mistress continues a stumbling dance, away from the agonising draught which is the cause of her panicky asphyxia. Her scrabbling hand finds and grasps a massive handle; desperately she presses down, and as the door swings outwards on discreet and ponderous hinges she follows it into the drizzly heartlands of her capital.

When consciousness returns to Prudence she is for some moments unable to accept the fact of her companion's absence. She blinks several times, praying that she is victim of a practical joke or a trick of the light. At last she snatches up the intercom and starts shrieking down it, at the same time beating on the glass panel, in her haste to rally help in this too awful emergency.

But the two men are no better able to understand what has been happening. Here after all are some of the hallmarks of royal kidnappings everywhere: a stealthy swoop, an efficient snatch, presumably a criminal genius. But the conventions of the genre have been imperfectly observed: where is the ransom note? What has happened to the statutory exchange of fire, without whose ensuing flesh wounds the good faith of the outclassed defenders must be left in doubt? Are there to be no bravery awards?

The abandoned members of the royal party spend many seconds in a state of paralysed nonplus, debating whether they are not perhaps overlooking a simple explanation or neglecting an obvious course of action, before they raise the alarm in the grand manner.

The Queen meanwhile, having made an undignified and jarring touchdown on slippery pavement, had sought refuge from the cold wet which agitated her so terribly down a flight of metal-edged steps, which had happened to be the merest few yards away from her as she reeled to her feet after that crazed leap into space. Lurching, stumbling, all but falling downwards, she found at last a thoroughfare relatively dry and warm.

Here her fit left her, while she leaned against a scrawled-on wall to gather her scrambled forces.

This was not quite her first experience of the London Underground and the tiled warrens that serve it. As a special treat she had once travelled all the way from Hyde Park to Tottenham Court Road on the Tube, with only a house detective and a lady-in-waiting for company (not counting Margo and dear Crawfie of course); the account of the occasion in her diary goes on for page after page, a thirteen-year-old's artless list of details, posters, uniforms, dirt, smells, the rails' anticipating crackle, the train's own wobbly cosiness, even though the event itself was a little spoiled by the increasing attention paid to the Nation's Darlings. They made the return journey by a less public means of transport.

Then three decades later, as Queen Elizabeth II she had declared the Victoria Line open, posing by the futuristic turnstiles for the benefit of a hundred photographers.

The first sixpence she was passed was repudiated by the

machine; only after an embarrassing delay could the grudging automaton be satisfied.

But this third time she explored the Underground's hidden life still less thoroughly; as soon as she was able she started to trudge along the subway, and emerged up another set of echoing stairs. The night air was no longer wet, though still quite chilly when one had not had a chance to dress appropriately.

By this time hysterical equerries were cruising the streets in official cars, desperate for clues. Not since Royal Engineers turned out with mine detectors to search for the Queen's lost watch had there been such a flap.

Along the dark side-streets and alleys which aggravated her poor eyes less than the orange highways the Queen lurched, past all-night cafés, past dustbins overflowing with hair outside the salons de coiffure.

In the course of her wanderings that night she was several times nearly run over by insomniac cars. Her education had been aimed at equipping her for the most probable royal eventualities, but couldn't hope to prepare her for everything. Inevitably it was strong on constitutional history, weak on kerb drill, so we shouldn't too readily blame her lack of prudence on illness. Although she hadn't needed to take a test of any sort, she was certainly a skilled driver; but in her present state she associated traffic lights as much with royal banquets as with the Highway Code. On formal occasions, red and green signals concealed in banks of flowers were used to give the menials their cues; so there was no guarantee that she would read the signs aright, when as now she wasn't actually behind the wheel.

Her higher centres, had they been working, would have regarded a less obviously dangerous incident as a luckier escape.

A television crew, in search of telling footage for a documentary on the homeless population of London, filmed her as she shuffled representatively past. Matter-of-factly the technicians recorded the Queen's ungainly progress, not observing that this particular vagrant, though dirty and dishevelled, was dragging along with her a huge handbag of creamy kid in place of the more usual creased carrier-bag.

At a later stage of the programme's production, more eloquent images ousted this remarkable snippet of celluloid.

So it was that Her Majesty, whose life since she had watched herself proclaimed Queen on a television in the drawing-room of Clarence House had been constantly broadcast and syndicated, was granted more privacy during this phase of her dissolution than a public figure has any reason to expect at such a time. It had taken press conferences and pleas galore to dissuade the newspapers from reporting Charles' career as a schoolboy out of existence; but in this her decline, all unknowing she received the grace of neglect.

Nor was this the only piece of good fortune to come her way that night. Fate decreed that she should be near a telephone-box when the rain started up again, so that she was able to take shelter without too much trouble. Normally indifferent as a gumboot to atmospheric moisture, she couldn't now endure even the lightest shower.

The compact and unfussy layout of the booth appealed to her immensely. Her first memories were of gazing up from the recesses of a cavernous pram past miles of space to the semiprecious bangles strung across its mouth, and only then to her Mummie's cool and smiling precious face. Then when the family moved to Buckingham Palace, she had always longed for a tunnel to cosier 145 Piccadilly, so she could sneak back there for the night. How then could she not be entranced by a lodging so intimate that she could touch opposite walls without even having to stretch? How much she preferred a few well-thumbed books—yes paperbacks even—to whole libraries of barren, beef-bound volumes!

Her dear Philip had never been able to overcome his sense of being oppressed by the ubiquitous high ceilings; their delicate mouldings and ticklish corners, accessible only to twelve-foot telescopic ostrich-feather dusters, crushed him with their spaciousness. So when the time came to redecorate his private apartments, he simply eliminated the excessive headroom, to fit in with his overall effect of a cramped efficiency below decks.

But Elizabeth felt that those born to the purple (like the Sandringham blackcurrants), singled out for an exclusive transfiguration (destined to be Ribena), must stick to that colour on duty and off, however distinct their preference for gentler shades.

All the same, there was never much doubt which was her favourite building in the world: what but Y Bwthyn Bach, the quarter-scale thatched cottage in the grounds of Royal Lodge, Windsor, her sixth birthday-present from the people of Wales? With its tiny opening windows, working baby radio, and price-less miniature sets of china and linen, it made a wonderful nest for Lilibet the little homemaker. But really, this booth was much better! Not comfy or warm down here on the floor, true, but apart from that . . . heaven!

The presiding shape of the telephone recalled her to a more practical frame of mind. She must obviously get in touch with her nearest and dearest; Prudence for one would be worried stiff.

There was no shortage of operators at the Palace, many of whom liked nothing better than to handle ("Your Majesty? Her Majesty, Your Majesty") the personal calls of the Royal Family. But the mighty handbag of course contained no money. Even in these bad days her credit was good, and if ever she needed actual cash her retinue would take care of it. When the collection plate came round in church, for instance, an equerry would render unto her a graven image of herself in blue green or brown, and she would place it in the dish.

What to do then? A few shredded circuits proudly retrieved and delivered a long-buried message. Reverse-charge call.

What could that mean?

A neighbouring ganglion ventured a synonym. Transfer-charge call. Which made no better sense. Her numerical skills being inferior to those of the average barmaid or darts-player, she couldn't in any case remember a single relevant number.

Perhaps the knowledge that emergency calls may be made free of charge had never found a home in that crowded head; certainly it didn't occur to the Queen as a possibility now. Instead she heeded that internal voice which had never in all her adult life stopped repeating its vow, but now once again dominated her consciousness.

I mustn't take the easy way out.

I simply must go.

I won't disappoint those poor people.

So with a struggle she opened the door of the phone booth, and forced her dissolving legs to carry her onwards.

Every step was painful for her now that she had lost both her glittering shoon. Perhaps some atavistic regal instinct directed her towards the theoretical home of her Court, St. James's, and it was surely her countrywoman's disposition which led her to its Park. It isn't impossible that the park was in some sense her private property, the keepers of the urban grove at some remove her employees; but she was past resenting their failure to open up for her. Waiving her rights of entry she collapsed outside the gates, without so much as a bench to prop up her slackened limbs.

Denied the consolations of her beloved chlorophyll, she drifted into a vivid haze of wish-fulfilment.

Condensing, her breath forms short-lived driftings of Scotch mist. In dream she snuffles the musky nearness of stags. Ornamental water, half-seen, swells and ripples into the likeness of a well-loved loch. The crushed and poisoned grass of her metropolis is become the austerely abundant bracken of the Highlands; curlews spiral overhead issuing faint cries, like police whistles. Solitary policemen call to their mates, and are answered on hoarse wavelengths as the city routinely misbehaves.

But when the thin blue line of flushed, fat-faced bobbies finally cornered her, she no longer made a very impressive monarch of the glen. She was far short of those twenty-point royals, to use the language of the chase, which she had tracked in happier times; she was defeated and drooping, her lopsided antlers secured by a square of printed silk.

DR. BULL: At some level, though, the members of the Royal Family are real enough to be left alone. More detailed revelations about their private lives drive private realities further and further underground, just as the film *Royal Family* merely streamlined the Windsor image. The media provide a convincing short-term substitute for life, but only a short-term one; and if the great glory of the image is that its emotional impact isn't diminished by knowledge of how it is contrived, its corresponding weakness is that its fixity can deform the living entity it seeks to embody. Certainly we shouldn't compliment ourselves on the value of our most shallow and ill-informed emotions, simply because they are in theory warm and positive.

What we have seen at work in the Royal Family is a sort of titanic adolescence, in which innocent self-reliance gives way to a neurotic attempt to justify the self to the world by way of an exaggerated attentiveness to others, but may eventually return to a more painstaking and considered self-sufficiency.

In March 1954 the journal *The Tailor and Cutter* honoured five-year-old Charles by placing him first among the best-dressed men of the year and paid him tribute in the tweedy simper of its house style:

"His Baby-Bow and Fawn Stalker, followed by his junior fashion for a d.-b. woolly, is accented this year by his adoption of a very popular style among older folk. The cloth-cap should always be moulded to a curved-peak effect and our picture reveals His Highness as being no square. His velvet-collared topcoat, too, follows a popular current trend."

Ultimately the only sane response to such stuff is to forget it; but this is a sort of forgetting which calls for a great deal of effort.

As an exemplary symbol of the Queen's plight, let me cite the odd fact that in the annexe designated as the dressing-room for her Coronation there was no sign of a mirror; the world demanded an image from her, but denied her access to it. On this occasion Bobo Macdonald, the Queen's celebrated Dresser and confidante, corrected the oversight, but in her life as a whole Queen Elizabeth has had to make or find her own mirrors the same as anyone else.

In the course of her life as Queen, Elizabeth Windsor has modified her initial girlish identification with her public role. At the beginning of her reign the prospect of having her own image on postage stamps so excited her that she motored over to High Wycombe to see the first batch, and she was tickled to death when first she spotted her cypher on a Windsor Farm milkbottle. But in subsequent years the crown monogram stamped on the breakfast butter-pats has become less of a novelty, and when specimens of a new Crown Derby dinner service were submitted for her approval, she had an objection to make: "I don't always want to be gazing at my own cypher."

Her eldest son made the same discovery of a liberating ennui earlier on in life; at the time of his Investiture, with its super-saturation of media coverage, he was heard to complain, "It's always me. I'm getting bored with my face." He was already on his way to that necessary indifference to his public life and persona to which Philip laid claim, when he said he could read about himself with the same detachment as he read "about some animal in the Zoo."

Philip's is a particularly interesting case. The inevitable failure of his public attempts to bring a fresh mind to bear on an institution which is sustained exclusively by its ripeness or its staleness (depending on your point of view), drives him to seek some sort of meaning elsewhere. His leisure activities as a sportsman are very far, therefore, from being indulgences; they provide him, whether the name of the game is skittles or big-game hunting, with ritual structures of competition from which he can derive a sense of personal worth. Ideally, the impression of movement, of getting somewhere, should be strong, the competition should be direct, and the danger high rather than low. Golf is understandably not popular with him. Boats and planes offer particularly rich opportunities for the obsessive assertion he needs to retain his self-respect; Philip (callsign *Rainbow*) has long since left humble machines like his Chipmunk trainer for more showy vehicles—Gannet, Canso, Solent, Shackleton, Constellation, Stratocruiser—and in fact once returned a Hovercraft to its makers with two sizeable dents in the bows, after a rip-roaring test drive.

Elizabeth's brand of personality on the other hand has never encouraged her to value personal pleasures very highly. Even as Queen she has remained dominated by notions of correct form and precedent. Her constant question has always been "What did my father do?" and she has modelled herself painstakingly on the examples he left behind.

Nothing has been touched; the country has been left just as it was when the old King died.

Only once, on 27 November 1953, is she known to have sidestepped a clear and acknowledged precedent. That was when Jamaican schoolteacher Warren Kidd laid down his linen jacket in her path. The Queen with a nervous smile walked round rather than over it, declining to play Gloriana to his Raleigh. His grin was alarming.

Still less as a private citizen does she revel in the adventurous and the new. As we might expect, her leisure activities are largely defensive rather than aggressive; they save her from boredom rather than provide her with arenas in which her will can strive for genuine sovereignty. It isn't likely that her struggles with crossword puzzles are in any way essential to her continued well-being. She enjoys the active sport of horse-racing at one remove as a spectator, but it is the administrative aspect, and particularly the gathering and sharing of expertise, which most appeals to her.

And yet even her modest devotion to the stable and the turf isn't immune to the unreality of her office. For it is undeniably ridiculous that one of the world's richest women should work herself into a lather, pounding the rail with a white-gloved fist and bellowing "Hooray! We've done it!" over the success of one of her race-horses, even if it is a ridiculousness which must compensate for many others. The Queen has had to acquire the knack of consulting only herself in her private life, which her subjects are able to take for granted as their right; she must cultivate a saving disbelief in the enforced shallowness of her life, ignoring as best she can the feeble orthodoxies which condemn blood sports or dancing on Sunday. It is ironical that a woman whose public existence is made a desiccating round of rituals and observances, which are treasured precisely because no argument can be devised to excuse them, must face so much pressure to justify and rationalise her private life.

To be revered merely for being, which in itself deprives your actions of substance, and at the same time to be called by your unthinking subjects to defend your personal doings, constitutes a life of the most schizophrenic stress. No wonder the Queen relished her pregnancies, which with unassailable perfection combined being and doing, and for a few short months enabled her too to feel that her every action was its own excuse.

How charming it was, how fulfilling, to devote oneself to one's body and its selfless greed, insistent little demands for honey and cream cakes!

To recapitulate on the Queen's progress, we might examine the wedding presents she received in 1947. The great majority were routine super-luxurious gifts, most of them thankfully exempt from the monstrous Windsor tastelessness, which would later devise for presentation to Eisenhower a coffee-table inlaid with a map of the D-Day invasion beaches. But two gifts out of the 2,583 exhibited at St. James's Palace have the courage to be different, the daring not even to try to impress.

In one case this testifies to a unique intimacy with the recipient; Bobo Macdonald, the Queen's Dresser and the honoured possessor of an almost telepathic rapport with her, does not need to go against the grain of her humble Caledonian instincts in an effort to dazzle. Her position in the Queen's affections is firmly rooted in the distant and less self-conscious days of Lilibet's childhood, and she is secure in the knowledge that her present of a wastepaper-basket will be properly appreciated.

Gandhi, though, had given away all his possessions except for a spinning-wheel, and so with his own hands spun the young bride a table-mat. In this way he fashioned a rare victory of content over form, and by an effort of will created something like a personal relationship in the most desiccating circumstances imaginable; even if old Queen Mary called it plain unhygienic, a "horrible thing." She thought it was a loincloth.

There in essence is my thesis, that experience and self-consciousness can win back a kind of innocence; but will Elizabeth Windsor ever manage it?

I make no apology for the jumble of images and anecdotes I have presented to you; it isn't easy to reduce such a complex of ideas and attitudes to a relatively simple form. Nor do I apologise for my analyses of the Royal Family's circumstances and actions; we have no access to its members as real persons, and can only speculate. We can only chip away at the myths that encrust them, and look very carefully at the roles we force them to play. It is only hagiography that kills its subjects stone dead. Thank you.

V

Not many hours after her discovery by the police, Queen Elizabeth II lay comatose in the dear surroundings of her home. Buckingham Palace is a house of many mansions; this was the Buhl Room, well accustomed to accouchements, and also to less auspicious emergencies.

Covering the Queen was one of the sheets which, as Crawfie the governess confided to a startled world through the pages of *Woman's Own*, had had their working life extended by the homely expedient of having their sides turned to the middle.

Having in terms of the classical model of disease passed through the stages of *arche* (inception), *anotasis* (development), and *acme* (crisis), there remained to her only *paracme*. An admittedly euphemistic resolution.

On any analysis her life must be despaired of; there was no chance of Elizabeth Windsor doing a Matthew Winkler and recovering with the help of intensive care (if in fact he ever had rabies, and not post-vaccinal encephalitis). Apart from anything else, the six-year-old Ohio boy had started a course of injections four days post-bite, while the English monarch of fifty-odd had pressed on with her engagements regardless.

Even homeopathy, championed and touted as always by Queen Elizabeth the Queen Mother, could prescribe nothing more promising for the patient than a hair of the dog that bit her, imperfectly translated into Latin and diluted several thousands of times.

Over the hours family groups gathered and dispersed in the half-light at the end of the room. Unobserved by the distraught

Windsors and Mountbatten-Windsors, one of the corgis cocked a leg over by the deep-green curtains, "using the royal we," as Margaret (mischievous elf) had once termed it.

Anne was not present as yet, but her verdict on the Mall kidnap—it was incredible, the sort of thing one can't believe is happening—or for that matter the Queen's reactions to her own wedding (I can't believe it's really happening. I have to keep pinching myself), pretty much set the tone for the watchers' comments. Things like this just don't happen to people who are walking history, personified events.

The medical team conclusively established the presence of rabies by means of the fluorescent-antibody test; but this didn't make the situation any easier for the family to accept. How had disaster come to strike down their dear one?

Her anguished relatives would almost rather the Queen was suffering from kuru, the only other disease that is invariably fatal; it is easier to accept as benign a Providence which penalises those who eat the inadequately cooked brains of their fellow men, than one which hands over to a preposterous death an overworked public servant out taking her dog for a walk—for a connection was now established between the Queen's tragic illness and a corgi that ran away after behaving strangely.

The previous history of the infection remained strongly resistant to analysis.

Messages of the greatest urgency were relayed to Philip, still on the other side of the world. Prince Charles was now Regent by reason of the complete incapacity of the sovereign; but his changed status brought with it no increase in decisiveness. He and his grandmother, with his aunt intermittently in attendance but too restless to stay for long periods, were too cowed and shattered to do anything but await progress reports, and to live up for once to the family's image in the national subconscious by drinking cup after cup of stiff brown tea.

Mary Spencer-Warren has expressed the belief that Buckingham Palace was in fact the spot where the first cup of tea ever drunk in the country was made, the year being 1665 and the importer of the pioneer leaves the Earl of Arlington; but the person most genuinely interested in such titbits of information was the one by whose bedside the tea-drinkers were wretchedly keeping watch.

The effect of the doctor's diagnosis on Prudence was extraordinary; she remained motionless for minutes on end, apparently deaf to what those around her were saying, and then launched into a bizarre fit, an improbable lather dripping from her jaws.

She was of course suffering from hydrophobiaphobia, also known as hysterical pseudorabies. In this state of pathological terror the victim reproduces all the clichés of the popular notion of rabies, not excluding barks and attempts to bite. A latent Calvinism was aroused in Prudence, and she indulged in an orgy of guilt. Her conviction that the disease had been transmitted to her by the Queen via the barley-sugar stick testified to a tortured regret that she had lapsed from the canons of hygiene, but also hinted at a deeper sense of shame. She knew that God was punishing her.

God was capable of anything; He had once sent a rail strike to thwart an ex-governess who was ruffling feathers in the Palace by going public. God nipped her second career in the bud. The unhappy creature had sought to supplement the (forgive her little joke) *royalties* of her books on child care among the Windsors, by reporting the grand events of the social calendar for a women's magazine. But her prefabricated bromides were shown up rather, when Royal Ascot was postponed, thanks to a rail strike, while her enthusiastic account of it appeared bang on time.

This comeuppance was regarded as piquant poetic justice by those who felt that a royal employee who blabbed was betraying a sacred trust.

Prudence was innocent of any such overt disloyalty, but she did have a guilty secret. In countless exercise books locked away in drawers, she had in her toiling copperplate accomplished the genteel apotheosis of her mistress' charm, consideration, and dress sense. Her intention had only been to prepare a volume for publication after her death, if at all, and she was doing no more than setting her affairs in order when, a little while ago, she sent part of the manuscript away to be typed. But now she felt she had called down wrath from heaven.

The two cases were treated in tandem by the team of doctors. They could do little for either lady, one being past saving and the other in no particular danger. The commoner put up a consistently more impressive show of hydrophobic pyrotechnics than the regal patient. Whereas the Queen sank into a garrulous semi-consciousness, Prudence was quite intractable; only Nurse Drinkwater, a huge and slow-moving Irish girl, could do anything with her. When Kaiser Wilhelm II at the age of four bit Prince Alfred and Prince Leopold savagely on the legs, it was a bad omen for Europe; but similar conduct from Prudence was infinitely more shocking. In due course one of her colleagues was unwise enough to address the Nurse by her surname, and in the terrific struggle which ensued Prudence somehow broke an arm. Up to that point her vigour and stamina had seemed actually to be increasing, and it was this fact, very far from characteristic of rabies, which finally alerted the medical experts to their misdiagnosis.

Nothing can be decided until Philip returns; no-one comes near him for organisational flair. A lady-in-waiting is deputed to write down as much as she can hear of the Queen's indistinct monologue, in case it casts any light on events

Rarely has a non-Windsor been privileged to hear such a long unscripted speech from the Queen's lips. Stage-fright deters her from speaking impromptu; even scripted broadcasts have cost her agony in the past, and caused her to leave half her Christmas dinner, out of worry, in 1957. As a child she found it easy enough to improvise; on a wartime Children's Hour programme she departed with confidence from the prepared text:

ELIZABETH: *My sister is at my side and we are both going to say goodnight to you. Come on, Margaret.*

MARGARET: *Good night.*

ELIZABETH: *Good night, and good luck to you all.*

But as an adult she has retained no such fluency. At social events her hands have often been so tightly clenched that her audience has feared her gloves would split.

In her prime, speaking off the cuff could make her feel quite ill. Now, though, she talks freely. The curse of her self-consciousness has lifted.

"How is the Empire?" she asks faintly. These were the last rational words of George V. His grand-daughter is not only being rational; she is justifying the enormous reputation she has earned for attending to detail and remembering the human, the significant fact. The balcony of the Empire has for some time been threatening to collapse, and Her Majesty is expressing the hope that repairs will be completed in time for the scheduled royal film première of Walt Disney's *The Rose and the Ring.*

But next moment her grip on reality slackens, and she suffers a delusion, much as George III in 1787 mistook an oak tree in Windsor Great Park for the King of Prussia. The mirage appears before her, suggested by a doctor with a syringe, of a republican with a humane-killer, and she shouts, "GOOD GOD IT'S WILLIE HAMILTON KEEP HIM AWAY KEEP HIM OFF!"

The injection takes effect and she sinks back onto the pillows. Just audibly she murmurs, "What makes people do such terrible things? . . . One ought to know. . . . I have so much to learn about people. . . ." Elizabeth has been praying for insight into the motives of ordinary people for almost half a century now, and still there are mysteries that elude her. Her diaries are filled with pleas for the faculty of understanding, and she strives in their pages to turn the mascot's engagement-book back into a day's worth of individual experience. Keeping a diary is such a comfort. A daily session of self-communion is part of the minimum requirement for staying sane in the job.

But it isn't sanity that is failing her now. She is undergoing a more thorough erosion, and she tries to find words for what is happening to her. "My head feels . . . all hoosh-mied up . . ." she manages to say. *Hoosh-mi* is a nonsense word coined by Princess Margaret as a child, and means (as a noun) *mixed food* of any sort, or by extension (like the similar words mish-mash, mess, farrago, hodge-podge), "disorderly jumble." As a verb it means *to mix up.* The inventive sensibility which was Margaret's mezzoforte as a child took her less far than had once been hoped. She peaked early, contributing a line to J. M. Barrie's *The Boy David,* for which she received the fee of a penny each time the play was performed. Her contact with the arts was never again so direct. Margaret liked her food well and truly hoosh-mied in those days, adding Force to her ice-cream, putting three spoonsful of sugar in her Bovril. Lilibet was more conservative; and when the war came she wouldn't willingly forgo her powdered egg, or any other sacrament of her rationed communion with a suffering people. The peanut butter, part of a food parcel from the States, with which little Margo spread her profaned wafers, she regarded as unfairly gained, hardly better than stolen goods; and would not be persuaded to try any.

The lady-in-waiting with the note-pad leans forward to catch the Queen's next words. ". . . where's Philip, oh Philip where are you . . ." Elizabeth in wifely distress unwittingly echoes the impertinent queries of crowds from the time when her arrangement with her Prince was not officially acknowledged. Given a relevant rumour and at least three weeks for it to become irrevocably established, the Palace Press Office will undertake to deny anything, from marital squabbles in the high homes of the realm to under-age drinking in remote public-houses. Whitewashed milk is even more unsettling stuff than white-washed coal; and it's many years now since the staff of Southern Railways, in its efforts to shield the royals from ugly truths, used any of that.

Even now the Press Office will only admit that Her Majesty has cancelled her engagements for the week.

The lady-in-waiting writes on: ". . . don't leave me Philip, don't leave me alone . . ." Philip's adventurous instincts have always worried Elizabeth on his behalf; but all she can do is give him a stiff little booklet, such as she herself is denied, inscribed To My Own Dear Darling From Your Lilibet (Passport No. 1, occupation Prince of the Realm), and pray for his swift return home.

They have had such wonderful times. She has been so lucky. She has such memories, of "Kosy Korna" and "Memories," the huts they used at Silver Sands beach club in Jamaica. A lemon roof and a blue.

Philip always knows what to do; he will help her to get organised. He will do what he can to take the pressure off her. People expect so much!

Philip will request on her behalf that Monday be kept free as a second day of rest. He will express her preference for tree-plantings over foundation-stone ceremonies. He will fight off the motorcycle escorts which block her from the view of her people. He will weed out unsuitable menus and defend her from all that rich food.

A three-course meal, plainly cooked, is the ideal fare. But some people can't say hello without giving you a lobster dinner!

Philip will look after everything. But where is he? It's not as if she can go alone. It's not as if she can go until he gets here. She couldn't stand it, not alone.

By now her voice is very faint, and the lady-in-waiting has to lean over to make out what she is saying. "I won't go through all that again," she whispers. "I can't face it. Do you hear?" Still fainter. "It's Royalty speaking."

Her Majesty's vision of the next world is turning sour; no longer does she see it as just another country to be toured. It is more like a session of everlasting detention, as she would realise if she had attended school. She sees a line of scarred desks stretching on to the crack of doom, each weighed down with red despatch boxes of one colour or another. Victoria and Albert are the furthest visible figures. The Widow of Windsor's bunched old frown is transfigured with joy as she works through her stack of documents, claiming a kiss for each signature. The Prince Consort does her blotting for her, his face still ablaze with typhoid fever. In front of them sits Edward VII, smoking a large cigar and throwing poker dice on top of a pile of greying papers. As a reward for his diligence, George V is treating himself to a session with the royal stamp collection. How quick are his movements, how sprightly his tweezers; and how clumsy he seems when the papers build up and he must resume work with his pen! Edward VIII, Elizabeth's favourite and unforgiven Uncle David, sits bored and flamboyant in casual clothes of extreme stylishness. The family's black-sheep and golden-boy is sipping a cocktail, leaving sticky rings, as always, on the state papers in his keeping; he holds in his other hand one of the double-decker sandwiches which were looked on by the staff as crimes against nature, when Mrs. Simpson tried to coax some out of the Kitchens. George VI relaxes after doing his boxes with a pastime which his brothers also favoured. He is making chair covers in petit point, though filling in the background is fearfully boring and it would be nice to have someone like Crawfie to do it for him. And now Elizabeth is due at the desk, decorated with a rotting clump of discoloured fibres instead of the usual deep-pink carnations, where her duties will stretch on into eternity. Her attendance here is in Philip's terminology more than an EP, engagement possible, more even than an MBTG, morally bound to go; it is an excruciating imperative. Here she must choose designs for her monumental clothes, and painters to portray her in them. Here she must mug up the travel books for endless projected tours, and deal with her hundred letters a day—not excluding the petulant and continuing correspondence from the lawful Queen of England, commonly known as Mrs. E. M. Ottewell.

You old folk, more than five thousand of you a year, who wait in pairs and singles for your telegrams; who are unwilling to split up or pass on until The Queen Is Much Interested to Hear that you are celebrating your one hundredth birthday or sixtieth wedding anniversary (or conceivably both), and sends you warm congratulations and good wishes; you centenarians, a few of whom will hang around for five years to form a further élite, after which your monarch's cheery wires become an annual event, and you've hardly time to read one before the next arrives; surely the second Elizabeth will not neglect her duty toward you? Surely she won't let you down?

The Queen's voice suddenly regains its full authoritative timbre. The lady-in-waiting barely manages to keep her balance as the patient roars:

"I WANT TO TAKE THE EASY WAY OUT

I SIMPLY WON'T GO

I DON'T CARE WHO I DISAPPOINT

LET IT BE THE EASY WAY OUT FOR ONCE. . . ."

Philip, when he came, was somehow able to cope. He took charge immediately, arranging the basic but so far neglected business of assembling the family; messages were sent on their way to distant Andrew and more accessible Anne. He also found time to hear progress reports on enquiries into the source of the disease, and to discuss possible ways of containing it. The proposal that as a precaution the Park wildlife be eliminated, right down to the smallest species of tramp, received considerable support amongst his advisers; but Philip felt unable to give it his approval. His long-standing association with the cause of conservation and the vital business of preserving the environment made it unthinkable that he should condone slaughter on such a scale, and he recommended instead that they should await developments.

This was far from an ideal solution to the problem, inasmuch as development in the case of rabies may take as long as two years; but it was at any rate a forthright and positive piece of procrastination, and it gave Philip heart to tackle his next and most difficult decision.

Philip reasoned that if the action demanded by the crisis was to be successfully carried out, Charles' position must be confirmed and enhanced; it was not enough for him to be Regent. On his orders, therefore, all fifteen documents of the Instrument of Abdication were presented to the unconscious Elizabeth.

Her high sense of duty had always been exemplary. It had driven her to cope with her paperwork at twice her father's rate, and it had ensured that her greatest pleasure of the Wilson administration lay in knowing more than her chief minister on the subject of Milton Keynes. Nor did it now let her down; it enabled her to triumph over the painful winding-down of her being. Preoccupation with her father's death had not stopped her from signing photographs for her staff before she returned to London, so why should preoccupation with her own prevent her from doing what was asked of her? Her coma remained unbroken; but firmly, and without trembling, her hand grasped the pen and traced that authoritative shape in the creamy spaces prepared for it. She clipped forty seconds off her uncle's record for the course.

Cardinal Crescence (see page 3) was lucky in his contact with rabies, in that his sufferings were brief; a dog strangled him in the course of its convulsions. Most victims of the disease suffer more directly and have longer to wait. Someone of Charles' sensitivity was unbearably conscious of this fact; and he was persuaded with less difficulty than his father had anticipated that the Queen's agonies must be abridged.

Constitutionally, the priorities of the new reign were the attendance on the Monarch of the Accession Council, and his Proclamation to the people from the symbolic centres of the realm, from outside St. James's Palace, from Charing Cross, from Temple Bar, from the steps of the Royal Exchange, from the Tower of London, from the balcony of the Middlesex Guildhall, and from there outwards obscurely through the shires to the great nations of the Commonwealth. But before he could contemplate any such ritual dances, Charles had to have his mother put down; perhaps the only area of royal experience not even in theory or in symbol entrusted to a hereditary official.

Father and son put on a formidable show in the course of their delicate interview with the doctors. They made it clear that there could be no Euthanasia Honours List as such; but the Royal Victorian Order has always been in the sovereign's personal gift, and was mentioned in this context as a possible reward for services yet to be rendered.

It was only after a great deal of heart-searching that the citizen's duty to his Monarch took precedence over the Hippocratic Oath; and even then, it was with the important extra stipulation that the mercy-killer's identity be kept a secret, even from himself.

The traditional method of putting the rabid out of their misery, by smothering, was dropped in favour of more modern techniques. Each doctor was issued with a hypodermic, but only one of the little cylinders was charged with the authentic Styx.

The Queen's time is running out, whichever of her thousand clocks—three hundred and sixty at Windsor, three hundred at Buckingham Palace, two hundred and fifty at Balmoral, a hundred and sixty at Sandringham—you reckon by; whether they strike slowly, with preparatory snores and groans, or swift as a Borgia; whether they are right up to the Greenwich minute or instead keep "Sandringham time," one hour early; whether they keep going for a year without being wound by the man from Frodsham's, like one of the Tompions, or only eight days; whether they give the age of the moon and high tide at thirty-two ports, like the "astronomical" clock of 1765, or attend more strictly to basics; whether like a remarkable Dresden specimen, they propel model bees round a porcelain sunflower, or simply allow sand to fall through an aperture, like the hour-glass on the Queen's desk; whether they are portable or built in, bronze or tortoiseshell, ormolu or marble; their message is the same.

The royal timepieces, though, have no real authority. They have only the right to be consulted (in emergencies or as a matter of routine), the right to encourage (the scrupulous making and keeping of appointments, the practice of consistency, achievement of targets, meeting of deadlines), and the right to warn (against wasteful disorder by the example of regularity). Having a near-monopoly on horological antiques never did anything to make Queen Alexandra more punctual, nor Elizabeth of Glamis after her.

But now Elizabeth keeps her last appointment. The medical team approaches the bed.

When in 1907 the Cullinan Diamond, astonishing chips of which would later form part of the Queen's inheritance, came to be cut, just this air of desperate expectancy surrounded the team of jewellers; but this time the peerless gem to be split was the Queen's own consciousness.

And just as J. Asscher of Amsterdam twice swooned during the crucial cutting operation, so now one of the six medics—though not necessarily the one whose plunger in fact squirted the Queen into another world, that would be too neat—passed out immediately after administering his injection; and a second time, when on waking he learned that the former Queen's name had indeed been struck off the register of the living.

Only her nails would go on growing for a little while; her scalp would push out a few more millimetres of hair. But though the new fibres would be less rich a brown than the lengths her hairdresser had attended to, she would somehow retain her dignity.

Being dabbed at her Coronation, on hands, on breast, on head, with the forty fats and spices of the hoarded chrism of the realm, was not enough, as things turned out, to insure her against act of dog. Nor when the Lord's Anointed went to her long home was the veil of the temple rent in twain from the top to the bottom, though a member of staff later declared that at the relevant instant, a heavy curtain in one of the North Side rooms crashed to the floor in a cascade of creaking plush.

Elizabeth Windsor is now less animate than any of the ticking treasures of which she has been steward; the unique Negress Head clock for instance, two-thirds life size. Tweak its right ear-ring and the eyelids flutter open, displaying the time in the pupils, hour left eye, minutes right; the left ear-ring will serve you as the key to a concealed mechanical organ, eight tunes on sixteen pipes. But tug at Elizabeth's ear-ring—left or right, it is all the same—and you will only stretch the elastic lobe, will feel only her congealing neck's resistance to your pull.

Those ears, scarred and pitted by ten thousand hours of choral patriotism, have now at last fulfilled their incarnation's quota.

Eyes cruelly overexposed to red carpet only now lose the lifelong green of its after-image.

Her face, having retained its smile through an unending barrage of flying tins, placards, flags and flowers (the camellia heads thrown with stinging force by the enthusiastic Portuguese being the most painful), is content to have others prepare it for sleep as best they can.

A brain that for decades has striven to master and retain every little shifting of the political balance gratefully relaxes its coils.

The head whose image in full face has endured a million stares laden with a million meanings and prejudices, and in profile weathered the blows of a million frankings, to assist her subjects' pleasures, to endorse their business, will feel no further pressures.

The unassuming celebrity who has been hailed in public as Li-sa-be-ta, as Queenie, as Happiness, as Brenda, as La Petite Souris, as Attagirl, as Queen Mam, as Lizabette, as Young Mrs. Queen, as The Fairy Princess, as Hullo, as Yea Betty Yea Windsor Yea Yea Betty Windsor Rah Rah Rah, has quietly taken leave of her people.

Charles had never felt so frightful. His only real experience of loss had been the morning when he found Harvey the Angora rabbit in a state from which no amount or quality of greenstuff could rouse him. He retired in extreme distress to his own apartments, and locked himself in; beyond which barrier we will not pursue him. Except perhaps to say that he spent a long time on his knees, and then sat abstractedly in an armchair while one of his Goons records blared from the record player at an uncharacteristically high volume.

Edward was listening to his new cassette of BBC-marketed sound effects; it was Volume 13, Death and Horror, which he was thinking of using for the soundtrack of some ciné films he and Andrew had recently made. Thirteen-year-old Edward's acting showed all the compensatory taste for the macabre that the family had been noticing, with mixed feelings of amusement and concern, over the last year or so; the film consisted almost exclusively of shots of him, caped and fanged, his young face screwed up into a demonic mask and his mouth afizz with mock-blood capsules, leaping at the camera from along corridors, from on top of walls, from behind gravestones. Lurid effects jostled each other on the tape; the initial four-second guillotining was followed straightaway by Arm Chopped Off (3″), Head Chopped Off (3″), and for the hat-trick Head Sawn Off (a full five seconds). The Queen Mother entered without knocking, heavy with news, just as number 10 Red Hot Poker into Eye, 7″, was giving way to the eighteen seconds of number 11 Nails Hammered into Flesh.

She kept her feelings tightly reined in. A lifetime of performing in public enabled her to mask her grief even from her daughter's son. She was calm as she sat ponderously down next to him, and took both his hands in hers before starting to speak. The engineers were getting Track 2 under way with an indulgent sixty-five seconds of the Mad Gorilla. As she spoke, Elizabeth of Glamis pressed Edward's hands between hers with a slow rhythmic emphasis.

Margaret was also surrounded by sound in her retreat; in her case a no less horrible blues raga that she had once adored, but now found beyond words irritating.

Her musical taste had always represented a reaction against Elizabeth, whose painstaking rendering of "Für Elise" could easily be trumped by a flamboyant "Twelfth Street Rag"; but now for a few moments Margaret was unable to find her character. So she switched the music off at the mains and instead built herself a towering Pimm's, adding in turn to the aromatic base a hefty slab of cucumber, the hide and meat of a monster lemon and a stalk of borage the size of a sequoia, before topping up with chilled citrus froth.

To alleviate her depression as she sipped, she picked from the shelves *Long to Reign over Us?*, the record of a 1964 survey on the royal image, and flipped through its pages; this soon had her smiling in disbelief at individual twitterings of the vox populi ("When the Queen is out of the country you don't feel quite the same"; "Prince Philip should come more to Maccles-field"), and above all a statistic from page 72 which always amazed her, retailing the news that (at that time at least) nineteen per cent of people in the North-East would rather see her than any other royal.

The phone rang, news undoubtedly; but she hesitated. She couldn't face having to be pious and solemn; perhaps she could make an excuse later on for not answering. Once upon a time she would have shifted the blame without a moment's thought; I was with Cousin Halifax (the Pinkle-Ponkle's successor as her imaginary playmate), she would say.

But things were not so simple nowadays, and she picked up the receiver at last.

Anne and Mark were out of reach for the moment, but music was colouring their environment too; they were at a nightclub, hanging back until the pace speeded up so they could dance. For a split second the prospect was perfect; there were enough people on the floor to provide cover, but still plenty of room to manoeuvre. They moved forward, eager to join the other swingers; but the whole crowd surged onto the floor at the same moment, and they found themselves inter-locking with the pelvic basins of strangers. Sullenly they disen-gaged themselves and returned to their table. They were still sitting there when the police tracked them down with the news.

For a long moment Philip was tempted to suppress any announcement of the death and recruit Mrs. Jeannette Charles, the Queen's "double," to take her place, instead of impersonating her for profit. Perhaps Mrs. Charles should be given the chance to learn at first hand that the hot seat of the English throne can be a cold and lonely place. He was dissuaded only by the practical difficulties of making the switch.

Philip turned his attention instead to the Press Office, which had been turning out anodynes pending his decision on the best method of informing the public. Bulletins, which had hitherto been playing tasteful variations on Her-Majesty-has-a-slight-chill, were allowed to progress as far as Her-Majesty's-health-is-giving-some-small-cause-for-concern, and from there to approximate by degrees to the truth; though it was a good long while before the grand nostalgic theme of Her-Majesty's-life-is-moving-peacefully-towards-its-close was properly stated.

The Earl Marshal's half-yearly ten pounds, though liberal, was never quite money for old ceremonial rope; and now he had a real and heavy responsibility to bear. It was up to him (though Prince Philip made a great contribution behind the scenes) to make arrangements for the funeral. More than three hundred thousand people had filed past George VI's body in Westminster Hall, but it was obviously undesirable to show-case his daughter's terminal rictus in the same way.

The omission of a Lying-in-State tended to encourage "mystery illness" headlines and all the associated furore; but this could hardly be helped, the illness being indeed a mystery, and was if anything a refreshing change from the usual nil nisi bogus de mortuis. The rumours had more substance than the usual ones. If ever the Queen gave birth, for instance, without portfolios of photographs appearing shortly after the placenta, the story would inevitably go round that the baby was incomplete, or an unexpected colour; but the illness rumours spread more widely, and would fade less fast.

The privileged thrill of immunity from death duties could do little to lighten spirits at the funeral service. The coffin, of seasoned Sandringham oak, reposed on the old-fashioned wheeled bier patronised by George VI. Prudence stood a little apart, her arm in a sling, chastened and a little unsure of herself. Windsor faces in their home surroundings of Cotswold stone took on expressions of vacuous bereavement, Windsor voices less easily sustained the tune of "The Strife Is O'er The Battle Done," and the tune (plus descant) of "The Lord Is My Shepherd" in the Scottish metrical psalm version "Crimond." The descant had made such an impression on the young Elizabeth that she sang it from memory for Dr. McKie to transcribe, and now here it was again to honour her.

Tradition demanded that the Lord Chamberlain, in token of the ending of his service, break in two the white staff of his office and lay one half on his mistress' coffin. But at some time in the century the custom had been slightly modified. Perhaps it was felt that the too melodramatic gesture unacceptably stressed trivial discontinuities at the expense of the changeless vistas of national life; at any rate the wand was adapted so as to unscrew. Even after hours of solemn solitary rehearsal, the Lord Chamberlain was unable to go through the symbolic motions without provoking a series of grating squeaks.

The Archbishop of Canterbury intoned the committal. Charles sprinkled Windsor soil on his mother's coffin from a silver bowl, as it sank through a cavity in the choir floor into the royal vaults, already populated by ten of her ancestors. In accordance with custom, bagpipes droned "The Flowers of the Forest"; whether the trumpets sounded for her on the other side was a matter beyond the competence even of the Master of her Musick.

Once the interment was accomplished, Prince Philip suffered some sort of collapse; though nothing as extreme as the incident at his first public engagement, the 1936 relocation of his uncle, aunt, and grandmother (King Constantine, Queen Sophie, Queen Olga) from Florence to quarters nearer home in the Tatoi Gardens of Athens, when he was sick into a borrowed top-hat.

He had in theory been on indefinite leave from the Navy

since his wife's Accession, and in his widowerhood he picked up the few trailing threads of that career; but at his time of life he could hardly expect to resume active service.

He had always hankered after relegation to the second division of royalty; had always seen himself as a Prince Midas, or at least as that George who had bent a solid gold knife trying to cut a pippin. He too had been thwarted as much as helped in his incisive and practical aims (installation of dictagraphs and electric kettles in underequipped Palace offices, preservation of wildlife, playing fields for all, optimal placement of AA call-boxes, encouragement of the young, improvement of rear lights on lorries) by the absurd distinction of his position.

Hence the passion of his tinkering, and his insistence on dexterous personal involvement: his elaborate scale model of Balmoral Castle, the plastic bubble he devised to shield the Queen on a Canadian tour, his dislike of having doors opened for him (I've got hands haven't I), his habit of designing the trophies he is to present, silver collar, Silver Wink. But he didn't when the time came easily give up the most expensive alienation in the world. He had expected to find himself again, once out of the limelight; but no self was waiting for him there.

Left alone with his memories and the largest collection of home movies ever assembled, Freeman of Acapulco and Belfast with nowhere to go, Philip looked out at the world from eyes whose ice blue, these days, was more and more reverting to water. He made mention much more freely of his contact lenses, which had been no part of his earlier, sporty image. Like bloody dustbin lids this morning. He propped himself up on the walking-stick given him by his old skittle team from the Methuen Arms at Corsham, the Moonrakers. But it cast him down as much as it supported him, for the occasion of the gift had been his wedding; and the inscription on its shank, "They are not long, the days of Beer and Skittles," now seemed too jocular, or not jocular enough.

Just over a week after the funeral the first batch of the

Australians arrived pale and shattered at Heathrow. The Associate Private Secretary's tactics, though successful from the medical point of view, had had some of the effects of a course of Pavlovian conditioning. The visitors were allergic to cake of any kind and loathed London Transport, Her and now His Majesty's Government, in fact the whole EEC police state. Only the glum residue of greed sustained them. Their feeling for the Old Country was now a generalised distaste; they thought it in particular a poor place for a convalescence. Their programme was as full and unmerciful as any Royal tour, leaving them no minute of spare time, and it rained almost without interruption throughout their stay.

A little more than a year after the Queen's death, her eldest son accepted the homage of a rapt and reverent kingdom at his Coronation. An illustrious date was selected in order to bolster the Sovereign's charisma with suitable associations; December the twenty-fifth, the day favoured by Charlemagne and by William the Conqueror.

Christmas was not usually an elevated occasion in the life of the ruling dynasty. Their version of the festival tended to be present-obsessed.

But when the law of your land makes provisions to protect citizens from being harassed by unsolicited offerings, while you yourself receive a deluge of unwanted objects, a sloth, nappies, three tons of toys, then Yuletide gloating over presents with knowledgeable thought behind them is perfectly understandable.

The midwinter cold took its toll of the crowds gathered to cheer their new sovereign. Overall attendance was down on the last Coronation, but casualties were well up on the previous 6,873; about fifteen per cent were ambulance cases. An average number of processing servicemen received bayonet-nicks from their comrades-in-arms as they turned street-corners in tight formation. Pickpockets were hardly more in evidence than they had been at the trouble-free junketings of a quarter-century before; perhaps because their sensitive hands couldn't properly function at such low temperatures. The shivering monarch's expert make-up simulated the tints of warm flesh for the benefit of the cameras. He had kept vigil all night, in accordance with the letter of the Coronation service, and could hardly keep his eyes open.

Bowing to a suggestion from his grieving father, Charles brought one of his subsidiary Christian names to the fore, and was crowned King Arthur II in robes of Dark Ages chic, tastefully interpreted and brought up to date by Lord Norman-Hartnell. Denmark chipped in with the gift of an enormous Round Table of bleached pine, unobtrusively complemented by one hundred and fifty smoked-perspex thrones. As if by magic, the threadbare Merlins of the Press produced lush copy out of thin air for months before the event, looking forward in fulsome terms to the dawn of a new era, an Arthurian era of charismatic and imaginative leadership. Fleet Street and the publishing houses, producing with great promptness shelvesful of celebratory pulp, were surprised and delighted to find that, even after so many years in store, the 1952 tinsel still had a certain sparkle.

BATHPOOL

PARK

(1 9 8 0)

The crimes belong to winter and to night, to dates between November 1970 and December 1975, and to hours between midnight and 5 a.m., but the trial takes place from June 14 to July 21, 1976, bright days so hot that the court rises from its afternoon session an hour early, at 3:30 p.m. No longer span of attention can be hoped for. The judge permits jury members to do without jackets and ties, counsel without wigs; and he expresses willingness to order a brief adjournment, in the event of the jury's concentration being threatened by sleepiness.

The crimes, and the preparations for them, were carefully planned so as to straddle the boundaries of regional police forces. Of the supplies needed for the final job, the sleeping-bags came from Northampton, the brandy from Nuneaton, the binoculars from Manchester. To link these scattered purchases with the theft of a van in Birmingham would be a feat beyond the powers of the police force, as evaluated by Donald NEILSON of Grangefield Road, Bradford. For the trial, 865 exhibits from the total of 3,000 amassed by the police converge on Oxford Crown Court, where objects, people, and words come to a passing focus.

The marshal focuses his waking senses on a cup of tea brought to him by the judge's butler. His sleep has been unrefreshing, and the day is already hot outside the windows. There is a film of sour dryness in his throat which resists the restoring action of the tea. The job of marshal was intended to give him a privileged view of the workings of law, and the quaint thrill of being paid his tiny stipend in guineas. And certainly he sits near the judge, high above the rest of the court, with what as a law student he should regard as extraordinary opportunities to see what goes on; but he learns less about British justice than about British weather, and British architecture's inability to make its occasional extremes bearable. There is a row of small windows high up in the wall which admit a theoretical draught; but there is no other ventilation in the court, and the moistness and heat are worthy of a sauna. In his morning-tails the marshal is more uncomfortable than he has ever been in his life, and his all-seeing position in court feels more like an exposed throne in which everyone, however little they seem to be looking, can see him beginning to doze.

He jerks himself awake again. The tea remaining in his cup is now cold and filmed with the fat from the milk, and if he doesn't get a move on he will be late for breakfast. Luckily for him, morning-tails are not required until a little later on, so he manages to reach the dining-room, in a dark suit, very shortly after the judge.

The judge has got as far as pouring milk over his cereal, and is casting a first glance over The Times. He offers a formal Good Morning, and on receipt of a similar one returns to his eating and to his reading. Though soaked in milk, the bran cereal looks stiff and unalluring as it moves, in judicious spoonfuls, from plate to mouth.

The marshal helps himself to breakfast and coffee from the sideboard before sitting down.

It would be wrong to say that the judge is reading the news, though that is how he would describe what he is doing. In fact he is running his eyes over the pages to reassure himself that the paper's hierarchy of news-value is being maintained. The world cannot utterly change, while a newspaper continues to resemble itself.

Somehow he has taken on the priorities of those he pays to inform him. A change of layout would affect him far more deeply than bad news expressed in a familiar format. A book review on the letters page would cause more intimate distress than atrocities properly displayed on page one.

He is reconciled to disorder in the world, it even confirms some expectations; but disorder on the page could only undermine him.

The marshal too, having unfolded his own copy of The Times, is reading the paper rather than the news. But the version of events which his eyes take in differs from the judge's in its subconscious assessment of live and dead material. The marshal turns every page until the middle one, habitually stopping for the Arts coverage, the London Diary, and any Letters to the Editor less than three column-inches in length; these are guaranteed to be light in tone. From there, having no need as yet to consult obituary pages, he goes straight to the crossword. He has faced up to the world enough to deserve some relief from it.

Today only one item snags the marshal's skimming glance and slows his progress down: the report of yesterday's proceedings at Oxford, which he observed at first hand. Although he feels foolish to be expecting such an article to yield up any essence, he reads it all the way through, unable to call back his attention, once he has parted with it.

The judge makes no such mistake. He knows, though only with the soft back parts of his head, that the case is notorious enough to appear in the Home News section, between pages two and five, as a matter of routine, and to be featured as front-page news on the day of verdict and sentence. Matters of public interest arising from it will be aired in an editorial or short signed article of comment, subsequent discussion on the letters page, the result of an appeal if any, in the Law Report. He will notice this pattern only if it fails to show up.

The marshal's is the quicker of the two reading-routines; carefully he tears out the crossword and slips it into his pocket, making a mental note to transfer it when he changes clothes for court. He will take refuge, when the day's session goes dead on him, in a smaller grid which is his exclusively. Now, while the judge finishes his second cup of coffee, he lets his eyes wander over the room. Its spaciousness ensures that it stays cool even on a day like this, and like the rest of the big house it has a heavy elegance of cream and clay-green. But the marshal, though a social secretary and not a bodyguard, finds his eyes drawn to the panic-buttons mounted on the impassive panels, which would summon help in case of emergency.

A whole set of procedures governs the security of judges when in Lodgings. The local police organise regular patrols through the park, and check the underside of the judge's car for explosive additions. And now the butler makes it known to the judge that the police escort for the official car is due to arrive in twenty minutes. He should be thinking of changing.

Judge and marshal retire upstairs to their rooms for the second phase of their preparations. The butler lays out on a hall table the judge's wig, the marshal's top-hat, and two pairs of white kid gloves.

The judge comes downstairs in his lightweight summer scarlet and spends the time until the car arrives standing restlessly by his desk, studying the papers spread out on it. The marshal, now in full morning-tails, with an oyster-grey tie to make sure that no heat escapes at the neck, waits in collapse on a chair in the drawing-room.

The judge's clerk stands ready in the background to scoop up the papers and take them without pomp to court. The judge will want to examine them again as soon as he arrives there, but in transit between lodgings and court he is a public object, and it would be improper for him to carry the actual trappings of his business.

The official car arrives with its motorcycle escort, the car's purr drowned out by the roaring of the bikes. The judge moves from the study towards the front door, his marshal falling in behind him, his clerk rapidly gathering up papers. With a bow, the butler presents the judge with his wig, and the two of them adjust it on his head.

The wig distinguishes sharply between professional administrator and ritual functionary.

From this moment on, he is a job personified rather than a person working. There is exactly as much human-being left in him as there is bread in a consecrated wafer. He doesn't any more interpret laws; the Law finds utterance in him.

No bow is bestowed on the marshal as he receives his gloves and hat. They are not to be worn but carried; they are badges only, and their resemblance to items of clothing is an incidental one. The gloves have been pressed quite stiff and flat; there are no stains of use inside the hat-brim.

These accessories correspond not at all to the marshal's size, as he has taken the trouble to discover, and even if they did would refer not to hands and head, but to his entire trivial office.

He follows the judge across gravel to the car, which shimmers in brightness. As he folds himself awkwardly to get in, he wonders with irritation what relevance there can be to British justice in formal clothes which don't fit, and aren't expected to.

Reaching behind him, he pulls down a folding seat opposite the judge and settles himself on it. Already there is dampness under his arms, and the gloves he holds are soon made sticky by his touch.

Nor is there coolness inside the car; the judge sweats visibly beneath his wig. Full judicial dress removes him so effectively from the world of men that his marshal finds it hard to start conversation with him. A presiding symbol of authority has no possible need for a social secretary, and inspires awe rather than chitchat. The wig, moreover, though not full-bottomed, enormously reduces the expressive potential of his face. It is impossible to tell whether he would welcome talk or resent it, and unwise in any case to presume.

Traffic has been stopped at the bottom of the drive to allow the judge's party effortless access to the road. The car rolls towards Oxford along a route chosen by the police and varied day by day. Car workers crowding the roadside at Cowley raise a cheer that may be ironic. Passers-by shout and wave when the convoy reaches the outskirts, perhaps mistaking it for something quite different.

Traffic has again been stopped in the approaches to the court, where a large crowd is waiting. Press photographers crouch on a low wall beside which the car must pass, competing for the best shots of the judge. A senior police officer stands at the foot of County Hall steps, and reaches out a hand to open his Lordship's door. Bows are exchanged. Then the superintendent turns briskly round and marches up the steps, setting the pace for judge and marshal to follow.

Inside the building, an aisle has been cleared between the gentlemen of the Press on one side and the public on the other, and the judge passes smoothly through. The reporters come to attention as the judge appears, holding their cigarettes and coffee-cups behind them out of respect, and make a ragged attempt at bowing in his direction. They receive a fractional acknowledgement from him.

The judge arrives in the haven of his chamber, where he can remove his wig for a few minutes and mop his face. He will be sitting for the rest of the day, so now he chooses to stay on his feet while the court is readied for him. His clerk enters, to supervise the transfer of papers to the courtroom. The marshal lays down his hat and gloves, and has no hesitation in sitting.

The judge examines the mail which has been addressed to him at court; this includes some glossy photographs of himself taken yesterday and sent on by the newspapers in an effort to court his goodwill. But mainly it is crank-mail, from people who have fitted this case's celebrated criminal into delusional frameworks of long standing. The Panther has become for them what the Ripper was for previous generations, and their pleas for attention can now be cast in a guise of compelling topicality. Their shared stylistic quirk is the use of the word because to mean both and and but: to express both casual and adversative relations. The judge runs his eye down the page until he comes across this specialised, near-technical usage. Then he hands the letter over to the marshal.

One of today's correspondents is a Grand Duchess Anastasia, who offers as corroboration a date of birth in 1919. Her attention is so frail that she is unable to sustain a sentence from the bottom of one page to the top of the next; the act of turning over the paper is enough to dislocate the tiny impulse of her thought. Her prenatal escape from the Bolsheviks is not explained; nor does her connection with the Black Panther ever become clear.

A knock at the door is the signal that Court No. 1 is ready for the administration of justice. The judge returns his wig to his head and straightens it, then walks the few paces across the corridor, where two policemen are posted, and into the overheated court. The marshal slips in by a side door and takes up his position on the judge's right. All stand.

There were dozens of brace-and-bit jobs altogether, through Yorkshire to Nottinghamshire and across from Lancashire to Staffordshire. The Post Office and the National Federation of

Sub-Postmasters in due course offered a reward of £25,000. Open war had been declared on a cornerstone of British life, a spokesman pointed out.

Hauls were as high as £4,400 and as low as £3, with several raids abandoned when things started going wrong. Neilson's rules were strict; they had to be, if he was to make do on his own.

1. On arrival, some disturbance beyond control. Do not proceed.

2. Can't enter. Try boring frame. No good. Leave it. Never make noise banging.

3. Inside. Awkward locks, etc. Reaches 4 to 5 a.m. Daylight approaching. Leave.

4. Find keys, unlock safe, empty cash, in and out without detection.

5. Entry disturbs occupants. No control from start. Leave at once.

6. Rouse occupants. Lose control. They take initiative. Leave at once.

7. Rouse occupants. We gain control and keep it. Convince them I'm in control. Never threaten to kill; instead: Do as you're told and you won't get hurt.

8. Guns. Far enough away from man, so cannot grab gun. Close enough to frighten.

9. Take coins, silver and copper. Hide away from P.O. Police think car used for job.

He liked the planning and the listmaking. He enjoyed disciplining himself.

1. Sub post-offices with living accommodation, so safe keys on premises. Nowhere near houses I worked.

2. Near motorway exit. People sleeping used to traffic noise. Don't wake easily. Also, police think car used on job.

3. In built-up area, but open land round it. Rougher ground the better. Get on water to cover escape. Defeats dogs.

He worked everything out on paper.

1. Ideal weather heavy rain and winds, not gale force. Dogs can't follow.
2. Bath before going out, in clean-washed clothes. Disinfected. No scent for dogs to follow.

He hoarded hoods and masks, cartons of survival foods, Ordnance Survey maps, telephone directories, and radios tuned to police frequencies. He built a press for making false number plates. He kept an Operations Book, and annotated his maps.

Lights go out 11 p.m. Dog barks at No. 4. Escape route this way. If boxed in here, no way out.

The attention to details of logistics, as also the vestigial use of <u>we</u> in a solitary context, derives from his time in the Army. The phobia about dogs, which he had seen used as trackers while on a tour of duty in Kenya, dates from the same period. Neilson's crimes were an extension of his military service.

If he was a law unto himself, it was <u>martial law</u>. It superseded the civil status quo in the area of his operations.

He had cried when he was demobilised, though he was never anything special as a soldier, and he never let on to his contemporaries that the military meant that much to him. But he did find it was possible to be afraid, and at the same time, to enjoy himself. He never saw any blood, gut hanging out, anything like that.

Nobody thought he had much go about him, he was more of a loner. He tried to make friends with some SAS troopers, but he didn't get far. The people he knew didn't have time for him. Other squaddies used to shrink their berets to look smart, but he didn't bother. His khaki drill shorts used to flap around his knees, and he wore a beret that was miles too big for him.

He was five foot six, so they called him <u>Shortarse</u>. His surname before he changed it was Nappey, so they called him <u>Dirty Nappey</u>, <u>Nappey Rash</u>, <u>Nipper Nappey</u>, <u>NAAFI Nappey</u>.

But unobserved he was carrying on a love affair with military discipline. Tracking, camouflage, and survival were his particular loves; and he took good care to fail his Bren gun course, so he could retake the ten weeks' training.

The Army took precedence over orthodox romance. True, he married Irene Tate in April 1955, but that was an affair of the pocket as much as the heart; the couple now qualified for a service allowance. The bride was permitted to collect the money, but had orders to save it and live on what she earned at the mill.

Neilson was no believer in the delegation of power in marriage. Irene got her white wedding but no guests, no reception. The groom, who wore battledress, was on forty-eight hours' compassionate leave; and the bride's mother and twin sister knew nothing about the wedding for another four months.

Irene's mother was never forgiven for striking Neilson, when she found out he had been breaking into her house while she was out shopping. She had thought it was burglars.

So the young couple embarked on their shared life alone.

It was a good marriage. He was a bastard to her but the marriage was a happy one. Everybody has their tiffs. She wasn't bad tempered, rather a happy person. She was a good mother and the best wife you could ask for. He did love her.

Neilson also loved his daughter Kathryn, born in 1960, but as she grew up he started to express his emotion by including her in his obsessions. He had for her the fierce tenderness of a sergeant-major towards a sloppy recruit.

The household at Grangefield Road came more and more to resemble a military unit. Neilson looked every inch a part-time paratrooper. The neighbours called him "Castro" because he always wore battledress, and <u>marched</u> down the street. He even bought a jeep.

You could see Mrs. Neilson in the back yard, dressed in jacket and trousers, helping to mix concrete or move heavy equipment. Kathryn was required to wear her hair short. Her father took her swimming at Undercliff baths, and the whole family went on fitness runs through Fagley Woods. Or they would wear uniforms and play games of military hide-and-seek; Neilson would brief his wife and daughter to stalk him through the bracken.

The Neilsons loaded the jeep with ropes and climbing gear for camping holidays. The Cow and Calf Rocks at Ilkley were a favourite spot for manoeuvres. They staged battles and stormed pill-boxes. They posed during war games for family snaps, carrying dummy guns made by Neilson from wood and metal piping, and stick-grenades improvised from soft-drink cans, with bits of wood stuck in them as handles.

Finding the shell of a jeep abandoned on the moors, Neilson set up a war photograph for the family album. He used smouldering oil-soaked rags to simulate smoke from an explosion, and photographed Irene, her uniform splotched with ketchup, slumping face down out of the vehicle.

There were elements of this regime which suited Kathryn poorly. She had only to get up from her seat and He wanted to know where she was going. If she ever did get permission to go out somewhere, He was sure to deliver her to her destination and pick her up again afterwards. She was looking forward to getting a job after her O-levels, but He wanted her to work for him at home.

Visits to relatives came under a ban, and no-one was allowed to call at the house. If Kathryn wanted to spend time with her favourite cousin, she had to make use of a code with her mother. When the coast was clear, Irene would pretend to put out the milk-bottles, and make a lot of noise rattling them. Then Kathryn would sneak downstairs and out of the back door.

Neilson found out about these expeditions when he came across Kathryn's diary, which gave all the details. He punished her with six weeks' detention, part of it in solitary confinement, part of it doing hard labour. Irene would bring food up to her room when she was confined there, but was under orders not to speak. Hard labour involved washing paintwork, stripping wallpaper, and moving a pile of bricks back and forth across the yard.

Family training kept Neilson in shape during the summer months, when the long hours of daylight made the joinery business almost a paying proposition.

It was also the season when bulky equipment couldn't be hidden under layers of clothes, and when gloves were likely to be conspicuous. When winter came, he resumed operations as a commando in an undeclared war. Ordinary life was suspended where he patrolled. He was a state of emergency.

He'd done his apprenticeship with simple housebreaking, which had satisfactions of its own admittedly. He did a copper's house once. No helmet, but got his whistle. That felt good. But with his lack of contact with fences, he was restricted to cash or near-cash, so post-offices became his exclusive target. And that way, the money he took was Government money. As far as he was concerned, he never robbed anybody. It was Government money and no loss to anyone. The Government could just print some more. He didn't want to rob old age pensioners. If he'd thought like that, he could have bashed old people on the head the way some lunatics do.

He never even had a decent holiday until he turned to crime. It was no fault of his he hadn't made any money. He didn't turn to crime to get a flashy sports car.

He didn't like bloody wogs in his country, paying nothing and getting supported. They shouldn't get taxpayers' money, his money. Blacks were ruining the country. There were Pakistanis who'd come to Britain and were drawing £100 a week from national assistance. He read about it in the papers.

At one stage a neighbour in Grangefield Road sold out to an Asian who arrived with a suitcase full of money. Neilson started thinking more and more seriously of a move. To Pudsey most likely. But he was careful not to transmit too much dislike to the newcomer.

"As far as Mr. Neilson was concerned, he took it quite well, really. There was no question of falling out over it and I am sure he realised that it was just one of those things."

Of course Neilson knew there were white blokes on the same game as well. He read about one who had been on the dole for ten, fifteen years. He was drawing dole or national assistance in different names in different towns. Some blokes on the dole were travelling round in taxis and were far better off than he was working all hours God sent. If the Government could afford to give Pakis social security money, he should be able to draw it too.

So when he raided a post-office, where layabouts went to collect their rotten cash, Neilson was attacking a social abuse as well as acting out a military fantasy. And he became very good at it.

The principle was, a shotgun a postmaster and a wife. You had a bloke in a detached house in bed at a psychological disadvantage, plus the time of three or four in the morning. He wouldn't be thinking straight. He was only in his pyjamas or naked. He thought of getting dressed and you were away.

To him, that was bloody simple. It annoyed him nobody thought like him. Everyone says, a burglar is a coward, but to wake somebody at night is not something cowardly.

He was scared to death when he was breaking in anywhere, but he enjoyed the freedom of being out at night. He could go anywhere he wanted, and nobody would interfere, nobody knew. At one time, there were as many as fifteen police task forces looking for him, the majority of them with dogs. He didn't do bad getting away from that lot, did he?

Throughout, even married postmasters were safe if they kept dogs, but they had no way of knowing that.

After a time it all became routine for Neilson. The system looked after itself. Whenever he took postal orders, he would take along the endorsing stamp too. Then he could validate orders with any date of the year in question, and cash them any time over the next six months. This gave him the chance, as he moved from one office to the next, to prospect for his next raid's ideal site.

The robberies were running themselves. So he started thinking of something bigger. Not just dribbles of cash from burglaries. Enough to develop his own business.

Trouble was, he needed a car for what he had in mind, and using vehicles was suicide. The police were always catching criminals through them. For the post-office jobs, he always used buses or trains. Still, there was no getting round it, so he made up his mind and set a date for early '74. And then what should happen, January 1st, but the three-day week, and motorway speed restrictions, and rumours of petrol rationing. A car would be too easy to spot now, with so little traffic about. He put The Plan on ice until things improved.

So the brace-and-bit jobs continued; but Neilson's concentration was no longer focused by novelty. He was still a good actor, but it was now late on in the run. Because of course the robberies were an act, and he was principal actor. When he put on the mask, he adopted a different personality. People saw him as the Black Panther and he didn't speak in normal voices. This was the same as a play.

Choosing his audience was no small part of the knack. His first bad choice was at Harrogate, on February 15, 1974.

He had with him, in a pack on his back, his usual minimum of matériel: sawn-off shotgun, two knives, brace-and-bit, two torches and four spare batteries, wire, two pairs gloves, lighter (to start fire if out all night), razor blade (to cut bandages if wounded), bundles of string, safety pins (essential repairs to torn clothing), ration block, hood and cap. He wore two synchronised watches on a single strap.

He had done two recces in a car, one visit to the shop as a customer, and one dry run at night. It took him less than ten minutes to get in.

He chose the son's bedroom instead of the parents', and rummaged through the clothes there for keys. Then he woke Richard SKEPPER and asked him where the keys were. In a cupboard at the bottom of the stairs, Richard told him. Neilson gagged Richard and bound him to the bed, then went downstairs to see. He told Richard to get some sleep.

After ten minutes, he came back to untie Richard's ankles. He spoke in short, sharp phrases, staccato-style.

"Can't find keys. Where are keys? You come, show me."

Richard was escorted downstairs to examine the cupboard. Sure enough, no sign of the keys. He made grunting noises behind the gag. Neilson led him to the kitchen and took it off so he could speak. Richard explained that his father changed the hiding-place often, so the keys were probably in his parents' bedroom.

"You get keys for me. Me watch at door. No noise."

"But they'll wake up."

"You go."

He tiptoed into the bedroom while Neilson waited on the landing. Mrs. Skepper was already awake. Richard crept past the furniture on his way to the dressing-table. His mother called out to him.

"Is that you, Richard? Are you all right?"

He answered "Yes" softly enough, but his voice woke his father.

Mr. Skepper turned on the bedside lamp and sat up.

This was a moment for Neilson to establish control. He moved swiftly into the room and used the voice of command: "Put that light out."

He wasn't getting enough attention from the people in the room. The woman was just staring at his face. She never even saw the gun. She wasn't abiding by the contract he was accustomed to establishing. She didn't consider herself securely threatened. She had gone from limp to brittle without ever being pliable.

"Put that light out."

Father and son were looking less at him than at each other; and there were two of them to point one gun at.

The gun itself was a less commanding presence than it had been a few minutes earlier, when the lighting was more favourable for theatrical effects. Then, he had let torchlight play along the gun-barrels as Richard awoke, but now he was losing initiative in the brightness.

"Light out. Put light out."

Neilson turned and tried a switch just inside the room, hoping this would kill the light if there was just the one circuit. Instead he switched on the main overhead light.

Mr. Skepper had a question. "What's all this? What do you want?"

But it was Richard who answered: "He wants the safe keys, dad."

Now that information was being exchanged without Neilson's participation, control was certainly lost. The gun would not any more be effective in a symbolic role. Its usefulness as a noun was over. It would be a verb now, or nothing.

"Wants the keys, does he?" replied Mr. Skepper. "Is he by himself?"

Excluded from the dialogue he had set in motion, Neilson attempted to outflank it with another. He glanced downstairs and called "Hey Mick."

An accompanied intruder, such as he now tried to present himself, could afford this moment of inattention; but a loner was risking everything. Mr. Skepper shouted "Let's get him," and swung his legs round and out of the bed.

He fell back into Mrs. Skepper's arms. Her first thought was that the shot had gone into the bed; then that her husband was slightly injured; then that he was dying.

Feet on floor, arms semiflexed. Shotgun pellets in folds of pyjama jacket, about 4″ round wound ($2\frac{1}{2}″$ wound). Hole in jacket 4″ × $1\frac{1}{2}″$. 220 pellets in abdomen. Track of wound downwards. Halo of pellet-wounds round main wound. Left ventricle of heart almost completely destroyed. Lacerations of lung and pericardium. No injury to hands or arms.

Neilson snatched up his bag and ran. He pulled off the hood as he reached the street and set off at high speed across rough ground. A little before daylight he made himself a hide in a plantation of pine trees, pulling branches over him as cover. He lay low all day, and emerged that night in darkness to return to Bradford.

He was profoundly shocked by the way the Harrogate raid turned out. Uncontrol had overturned all his plans. In his mind, after he had thought things over, was a picture of a tussle over the gun. The postmaster grabbing the gun by its barrels, jerking it in his grip so the safety catch was tripped forward, into the Off position, then using the gun as a rope to pull Neilson towards him. The tug-of-war forcing Neilson's gloved finger against the trigger, so the trigger pulled his finger not the other way round. More like an assisted suicide than anything else.

All the same, he kept Panther activities to a minimum. But when the days got shorter and the clocks went back, he was just as short of money as before; and so he went on another raid. He knew what had gone wrong at Harrogate: the man had got in reach of the gun. This time he would make sure of success, by choosing his ground with extra care. He decided on the sub-post-office at Higher Baxenden, a village suburb of Accrington, because he had been impressed by the postmaster as a nice, pleasant bloke.

He didn't take time to think that deference and willingness to oblige might be part of a shopkeeper's stock-in-trade, not automatically the core of his being. On the basis of one visit to the shop, he cast the postmaster as a young family man, whose priority would not be the monies entrusted to him.

A young bloke would think of the kids instead of having a go.

Two things about Mr. ASTIN were unsuspected by him, though theoretically they cancelled each other out in their likely effect on Mr. Astin's behaviour. One was that he was just as much an ex-serviceman as Neilson, having spent time in the Royal Marines. The other was that, also like Neilson, he had worked as a joiner, but had sustained serious leg injuries in a fall from a roof five years earlier. His move to being a postmaster was prompted by this accident; he still hobbled about, after all this time, and had undergone an operation to amputate a big toe only days before the raid. He was having trouble sleeping.

Neilson arrived by train at Accrington at about 10 p.m.; he had with him his usual stock of equipment and a shotgun, plus a .22 on a lanyard around his neck. This was in case of dogs. He walked from the town centre up the hill towards Baxenden, three or four miles away. He lay low till about 1:30 and then started to work round to go up to the rear of the post-office. He used the brace-and-bit method as at Harrogate, drilling a hole in a window-frame and then slipping the catch with a knife, but couldn't find any safe keys downstairs. He cut the telephone wires.

He got about half way up the stairs when he found they creaked. To make less noise and have more feeling in his feet, he took off his boots and put them outside the window. He went down on his hands and knees and felt his way into a bedroom, which turned out to be a girl's. The boards on the landing creaked under him. He moved towards the main bedroom at the back.

Missing toe or no missing toe, Mr. Astin came briskly to

meet him. He had no business being there, but there he was without warning, in his pyjama jacket. It was no good using the voice of command from a crouch, so Neilson stood up and said, "Quiet." Mr. Astin, not a small man, then threw him across the landing and into the bathroom, where he landed heavily on one knee.

The man was blocking the doorway. There was no other exit. If boxed in here, no way out.

Control was very far off by now, capture very close. Scrambling to his feet, he saw an object about three foot long being handed to the postmaster, and heard a woman's voice saying, "Here, finish him off with this."

It was in fact a Hoover that Mrs. Astin had picked up from beside the wardrobe, but Neilson had no way of knowing that.

Mrs. Astin from just inside the bedroom saw a flash and heard a shot, Susan Astin from her room heard two shots separated by about thirty seconds. Mr. Astin managed, in spite of a massive shoulder wound, to push Neilson downstairs, before collapsing against the wall.

Neilson landed on his feet and ran from the house at speed. When he reached the garden wall he realised he had left his boots behind, and had to go back and pick them up from outside the window. He jumped over the back wall and kept going till daylight, then lay low in hiding for the rest of the day.

Reviewing the fiasco at Higher Baxenden, Neilson felt oppressed to the point of persecution by bad luck. This time Control had passed from him before he knew it. He had had no chance to delay its going. There had been no time for him to showcase the gun, the pledge of his seriousness as a criminal.

Recollection presented events to him as cinema, with time manipulated to conform with what must have happened.

He saw himself feeling his way across the landing on all fours, with every faculty focused on making no noise. He saw the man appear suddenly in front of him, big as a bear. He saw himself without transition in the bathroom, seeing in silhouette a large long object being passed to the man. He saw himself struggling to fire a warning shot into the ceiling. Fumbling for the safety catch. Looking down to make sure. Pointing the barrel upwards. Becoming aware only as he fired that the man, still outside the bathroom when last seen, was now on top of him.

He saw himself falling again as the man's right arm came across to clutch the wounded shoulder. He saw his hand finding the .22, now loose from its position in his waistband. And he heard the .22 going off when his elbow hit the floor. By this time the man had spun right round and had his back to Neilson, so the bullet entered the inner right buttock, travelling forward and upward, at about 30° to horizontal and a little to the right.

Neilson was radical in his willingness to change mistaken elements of his schemes. In early days he had taken up the habit of changing patterns at random to confuse police. He would adopt a trademark for a few jobs, taking a pocket radio, say, and abandoning it nearby, or ransacking every drawer in the house. And he would drop a habit as soon as it was established as a common denominator.

It kept him on his toes.

But now much more would have to change. His next venture would involve a complete rethinking of technique. This time it wouldn't be a post-office with living accommodation. This time he would do the job in the early evening, at close of business. He would drop the accident-prone shotgun in favour of the .22. There would be no question of getting in and out undetected; he would surprise the postmaster, tie him up, and use his keys to open the safe.

Neilson was no longer keen to put his Control to any great test. Shaking off the jinx was his prime concern. His ideal subject wouldn't any more be a married man kept from self-destructiveness by warm ties with a young family; his record as a judge of this type was poor. His ideal postmaster would be older, and perhaps even frail, with a slow reaction time and no love of risk.

He would be Sidney GRAYLAND, of the sub post-office, High Street, Langley.

The post-office was seedy and tattered, soon to be demolished. Before the raid, Neilson saw only Mr. Grayland in the shop, and was impressed by his feebleness; when in fact it was Mrs. Grayland who was in charge. Sidney, whose health had suffered during his years in German prisoner-of-war camps, had been giving some help in the shop since 1972.

The couple's routine was perfectly constant and easy to observe. They lived about a mile away, and garaged their car in a ramshackle lean-to behind the shop. The post-office counter closed at 5:30; the premises were locked at 5:45. A postman in a van would arrive soon afterwards to pick up the mailbags of packets, parcels and registered letters. Mr. Grayland helped with the mailbags while his wife closed her accounts and balanced the books. She would mail the accounts to head office by way of a nearby postbox, cleared nightly at 7:00.

Neilson saw none of this. The only part he observed was Sidney's leaving the shop by the back door to turn off the water-supply to the toilet in case of frost, and collect the car from the lean-to. Neilson had no idea that he then drove round the corner, to the street side of the shop, to pick up Mrs. Grayland and do the final locking-up. Nor did he look closely enough at Sidney's exit, or he would have realised that the back door was reached through a primitive storeroom, full of furniture, stationery, and bric-a-brac, but not equipped with electric light.

It was easy for Neilson to insert himself into the Grayland schedule. He arrived a little before six on November 11, hopped over the fence and put his pack down by the back door. The car was still in the garage, so he slipped his hood on and waited for the approach of the postmaster. He wore rubber gloves. He had the .22 in his right hand and a torch in his left, with a plastic bottle of ammonia taped to its handle. This of course was for use against dogs.

Then he realised he would risk being seen through the bay window, when the postmaster turned the light on, unless he stood right up against the door. The doorstep was too narrow for him to stand on without losing his balance, so he was leaning with his back against the door, trying to decide where exactly to position himself, when it opened.

Although Neilson was armed and superfit, he depended so exclusively on planning and forethought that Mr. Grayland, though just as little prepared for events, had the advantage for more than a second.

Neilson managed to spin round and recover from his near-fall, but was immediately dazzled by Mr. Grayland's torch. He jabbed forward with his right hand in an effort to smash the bulb, but had his own torch-hand, the left, grabbed by Mr. Grayland. The torch, with the plastic bottle attached, was bent back towards him, and a jet of ammonia, forced from the bottle by the sudden pressure, sprayed across his knitted hood at eye level.

Blinded by surprise, by torchlight, and finally by his own ammonia, Neilson lashed out with everything he had.

The gun went off. Somehow in the dark the bullet found its way below Mr. Grayland's navel, passed twice through his intestines and severed his abdominal aorta. Neilson struggled to remove the ammonia-soaked hood and stumbled towards the door. Boxes and display racks dislodged by Mr. Grayland as he fell prevented its opening more than a couple of inches. Unable to see what was causing the blockage, Neilson turned round instead. He would have to make his escape by way of the shop.

As he hurried in this direction, hands outstretched in front of him, he ran into someone.

Mr. Grayland was by now lying on the floor by his lower denture and his spectacles; it was Mrs. Grayland with whom collision occurred. She had heard noises she interpreted as Sidney tripping and falling, and was coming to see if he was all right.

Encountering his fourth unwelcome surprise of the evening, Neilson had no reason to guess that he was now dealing with a middle-aged woman. Why with his luck shouldn't this be a professional wrestler? It wasn't a sort of fighting he relished at the best of times, with no scope for superior tactical intelligence.

He ended up on top of his attacker. He lashed out with the hand that held the gun, hissing "stay still"; he needed peace and quiet if he was to tie this person up, and so escape. He managed to fetch a bundle of cord out of his pocket, but the person beneath him started struggling and trying to get up. He lashed out again, and again he hissed "stay still." He managed to tie one wrist with the cord, but the person kept on struggling, and even tore the dimpled fingertip from one of his rubber gloves. "Keep quiet," he ordered. The person was being unrealistic; the person's wish to get up was just ungrateful in the circumstances. Neilson could only leave when the person was unconscious or safely trussed, and struggling didn't help a bit. He lashed out two or three more times, until he got the silence he needed.

Neilson dashed into the shop in search of a tap to rinse his eyes. He didn't find one, but continual blinking eventually cleared his vision. His breathing rapidly returned to normal.

He didn't even need to look around. There were two bundles of notes in plain sight beside the safe. He didn't want to go out the front way with the money, so he went back through the storeroom and cleared a space round the back door. On his way out he picked up his hood, bleached in streaks around the eye-holes.

Collecting his pack, he made straight to the canal to wash his eyes, and from there on foot to the caves at Dudley.

His eyes remained swollen and painful for some time, and Dudley was a good place to hide up. From the hill behind the Zoo he had a clear view over a large area. The caves had many exits, and there were several possible escape routes through the woods behind him. There were also the two longest canal tunnels in the country, which he had considered incorporating into future schemes.

But above all he needed to take stock. Three raids had gone terribly wrong, in three quite different ways; and scrupulous changes of plan had done nothing to eliminate the gremlins. He now saw he had been relying on precedent to pull him through, and it had failed him. He had only been changing details. Now he would have to rethink every assumption. The whole bloody lot.

Police activity was at an unprecedented level. Panther had to disappear.

He was fit but getting older. Thirty-eight was a good age to retire. All the same, he'd have to give the training everything he'd got, if he was going to make a go of the next job. The final one.

This was the job for which he had made The Plan a year before, the one which the three-day-week had forced him to shelve. It followed that the subsequent disasters were a side-effect of the energy crisis; and Neilson had no hesitation in blaming the deaths of the postmasters on the emergency measures taken by the Heath Government. But The Plan was a long way from dead. In 1973 he had rented garages in Nuneaton, Birmingham, and Northampton for use as supply dumps and storage areas for stolen vehicles. There had been no reason not to renew the leases as time went by. All he was waiting for was a winter's night with no snow and a new moon, and enough traffic to draw attention from one particular car.

By doing something radically new he would shake off the disasters which dogged him. He would smell so different that ill-luck would never pick up his trail. 1974 had been a washout. 1975 would be the year to make it big. Not just dribbles of cash. Enough to pack it all in. Enough to retire on. A golden handshake.

It was going to be a rush job all the same, there was so much to co-ordinate, but he hadn't thought of anything else. He kept reading in the papers about Pakis getting national assistance, and that turned the screw a little more. He didn't like doing nasty things to get money, and this was the worst. But if you have a reason it makes it easier.

He had been doing research on a casual basis for more than a year. His chief resource and home-from-home was at Bathpool Park. It wasn't his only bolt-hole, but it was his favourite. He'd been doing pack and distance training around Bathpool when he'd noticed a footpath along the railway. The path went past a concrete drain area and he came to an electricity substation. As he approached it he heard a great roaring noise from under his feet. He found it was coming from a manhole cover, not quite flush with the ground. He raised the cover and saw a ladder going down into a shaft.

He decided to come back with a torch and make a full exploration.

He lowered himself down the ladder while the water roared resoundingly below him. The drainage complex, excavated by a workforce of three thousand some ten years ago, was incredibly vast. It wasn't any too clean or dry, but the air was good. There were ladders and ledges, ventilation shafts, tunnels, crosstunnels, dry culverts, and a subterranean canal. It had even more possibilities than Dudley, and Neilson was quick to build them into The Plan.

There was nothing habitable in any conventional sense about the complex. But Neilson cleaned it up a bit and made the place his own. He had no objection to an unfussy billet, and his manner was almost house-proud as he did the shopping for his final job.

Brandy, binoculars, tape-recorders, torches, batteries, sleeping-bags, sponge mattresses, survival blanket, plastic sheet, polythene bags, Dymo-tape, sticking-plaster, writing pads, pens, paint and brush, wire, fasteners, spanners, socks, food, thermos flasks. He kept everything in the car for the meantime, in plastic bags and collapsible suitcases.

His target was a detached house in Highley. There was a corporation estate across the road from it, with easy access from the rear. He thoroughly familiarised himself with the house till he knew it like the back of his hand, inside and out. He climbed the staircase again and again till he could be sure of keeping the creaks to a minimum. That was by day. Then he did a night run.

For his preparatory sorties he commuted by train from Bradford to Nuneaton, and then picked up the car from his garage there, rented in the name of B. Ware. On his drives to and from Highley he observed every speed limit and every last rule of the road.

The night of the actual job was no different. 14 January 1975. Ideal weather. Heavy winds and rain, not gale force.

He arrived later than he intended. A plastic sheet covering some window-frames stacked behind the house was making a grand flapping noise. He went through the unlocked back door of the garage to the inner back door of the house. He didn't need the brace-and-bit. He removed the screws from the lock, took off the handle, and turned the spindle with pliers.

He checked the kitchen one last time to make sure there were no dog bowls and no tins of dog food. He cut the telephone wires and crept up the stairs. The boards on the landing creaked beneath him <u>as bloody usual</u>.

<u>The public gallery</u> is very full; the crowds have waited some long time for their seats, and are impatient for drama. Quite properly, they want a good purging, and the action in front of them is too mild and matter-of-fact to bring one about. They feel cheated that so much of the case seems to lie in the past, in the detailed statements, strongly stressed by the prosecution, made by Neilson at Kidsgrove police station after his arrest.

In a way, everything happened so long ago; but look at it differently and it's all a good way off yet. Anyhow, revelations are so long in coming that they might as well not bother.

Perhaps it was a mistake to be expecting so much.

It's like watching sport in the flesh when you've got used to TV. You have to work much harder to enjoy yourself.

It's all a bit dry really.

<u>The press gallery</u> is equally full, but nobody here has unrealistic expectations. There is easily enough drama in a day's sitting to make a full-page spread, even if you don't think so, it's there if you know where to look. <u>Neilson hesitated. A woman behind me tightened her grip on the gallery rail. "Go on," she breathed, "oh just go ON."</u>

The newspapers have been involved in this case from the egg. The genre of the crime, the victim, the method, all were suggested by the press. Several nicknames were invented for the criminal by Fleet Street, including the one which stuck.

The idea of kidnapping a member of a wealthy family came from the May 1972 number of Reader's Digest, which carried an article on the Barbara Mackle case. But Neilson so enormously improved the hidden-victim technique, which had ended in fiasco in America, that he was able to carry out the entire operation single-handed. His version was also designed to eliminate the danger of the ransom money being bugged, though as things turned out, the plan never got that far.

In the same month the Daily Express pinpointed a suitably wealthy family, and even supplied the address. The owner of a successful coach firm in the West Midlands had died two years earlier, and his will had come as a shock to his wife, living apart since 1941, for it mentioned sums in the hundred-thousand range, while she had been receiving maintenance of two pounds weekly. She had been content with this because she had only known George Whittle before his great days, and knew nothing of his subsequent prosperity. Reading that George had settled large gifts on his "other family"—£70,000 on Dorothy, who had changed her name to Whittle when she had moved in, £107,000 on Ronald, 28, and £82,000 on Lesley, 14—she got in touch with them. When they offered only to resume the £2 maintenance, she took them to court and won a settlement of £1,500 a year instead. The newspapers, in an effort to heighten the moral issues involved, portrayed the Whittles as unmistakably affluent. It was not in the interest of the Express, as an entertainer of the public, to point out that the gifts had been intended to avoid death duties and so enable the family firm to carry on; that the money represented the assets of a business rather than personal wealth; that the Whittles lived in no great style.

Neilson judged them to be snooty and stuck-up. They weren't nice, getting their money from someone who didn't deserve it in the first place.

As a matter of fact, Donald Neilson had wanted to build up his own business much as George Whittle had, and it remained his long-term ambition to set up on his own. After selling door-to-door, salvaging metal, and driving for a cab firm, he set up as a joiner. He put his best into everything he did. But he didn't have capital behind him, and the joinery business never amounted to much. In the winter months it dwindled to nothing.

Further guidance in planning came from a book by two Fleet Street journalists called "Murder in the Fourth Estate," which described the kidnapping of Mrs. Muriel McKay in December 1969 for a ransom of one million pounds. Again there was more than one person involved, and again the criminals bungled amazingly, mistakenly seizing Mrs. McKay instead of Mrs. Anna Murdoch, whose husband was a fully-fledged press magnate rather than an executive like Mr. McKay. But the police blundered too, through incompetence and unpreparedness, and the outcome of the kidnap, Mrs. McKay's death, was a collaborative one. The book covers these aspects of the case in detail, and Neilson studied it thoroughly. It also deals with the psychological pressure on the McKay family and the part played by the Press, but these concerned him less.

The police made such a balls of it and he worked on the principle of learning from their mistakes.

One fine idea which he adopted, again refining it out of all recognition, was the phone trail, pioneered by the Hosein brothers around the roads of Hertfordshire and Essex during January and February 1970. Phone booths are public facilities, but the system can be used for private purposes; messages can be left in a series of booths so that the person with the ransom, following the messages from place to place on a strict time limit, can have no way of informing the police in advance of the final location of the drop. Any police presence can also be spotted by the kidnapper if he takes up a position somewhere along the trail.

This was it, the only serious crime one man could do on his own, a kidnap.

The newspapers had done a lot to build up his confidence. They had already supplied him with a series of impressive nicknames. Handy Andy and The Phantom date from the time of the first post-office burglaries. His handiness was beyond doubt. Several times he was able to search clothing in an occupied bedroom, and only once in his entire career did he wake a sleeper without meaning to.

He wore dark gym shoes and he was ever so light on his feet. He made no sound at all when he moved.

The Phantom bit came from his elusiveness. A witness at the scene of one early raid swore that this intruder, this total stranger, leaped down the stairs in the dark in two great bounds, touching the steps only once in the middle. He was fantastically agile!

Red Shadow had a brief vogue in January 1971, when a shopkeeper was nudged awake by a figure wearing a wine-coloured boiler-suit, pillar-box-red hood, reddish rubber washing-up gloves, and red rubber-soled boots. His voice sounded West Indian. He was carrying a red rubber torch, and had a red holdall downstairs waiting for the post-office cash.

But Black Panther was the name that stuck. It had associations with radical politics in America, but it had plenty of domestic mileage left in it. You can have all the sensational-developments in the world, but with no headline you've got nothing. But if you've got a handle and no news you're still in business.

Having improvised the nickname, the Press soon published a rationale for it.

P—Post-offices

A—Armed with shotgun

N—No apparent accomplice

T—Timing: early morning

H—Hooded intruder

E—Entry: drills window frame

R—Rouses occupants for keys.

Commander Morrison of the Yard tried to bring Sewer Rat into currency, after the discoveries beneath Bathpool Park, but nothing more was ever heard of that. Co-operation between police and press was less than nil at the time, and <u>Black Panther</u> was here to stay.

There was something Neilson liked about the name, at first. A cat against dogs; that was it. So he bought Kathryn a statuette at Blackpool one year, a little ceramic model of a panther, and she kept it on top of the sideboard. Later on he moved it to a drawer instead. By that time the publicity was out of hand. They wrote anything they felt like. They were only concerned in painting a black picture; the truth didn't enter into it. They hadn't any idea what he was trying to achieve.

He kept cuttings about the Panther when he thought he could learn something from how the police reacted. Or anytime he might have made a mistake. But that was research; he wasn't stuck on himself like some people. He kept anything at all about the police mucking up, not just the Panther ones.

The police use of dogs continued to obsess him; he borrowed a book on bloodhound behaviour. If you plan for bloodhounds you won't have any trouble with Alsatians.

But he was more your practical sort of lad than the studious type, and his research was imperfect. Only when it was too late, for instance, did he think of the Press as an agent with its own priorities. Or that press and police could hamper each other, though this was made clear enough in the McKay book.

He could make a list OK. But he was no great shakes at plotting relationships.

The complex relationship of police and Press deserved his attention. The conflict is inevitable between a <u>scoop</u> mentality and an <u>arrest</u> mentality, with their different priorities and different levels of public accountability. A <u>scoop</u> is a short-term thing, the momentary triumph of a competitive alertness; an <u>arrest</u> is the end-product of a massive co-ordinated effort. The two mentalities have complementary strengths and weaknesses. A scoop is still a scoop even if it has to be retracted in small print the next day, because the sale of a newspaper isn't reversible. But an arrest must <u>stick</u>, or it isn't any good. But then again, a police force can survive patches of bad luck and slow progress, while a newspaper will suffer unless it pounces on a regular basis.

Police and Press are working opposite transformations on the facts. The police force aims to provide maximum reassurance, while the Press is all the time extracting maximum excitement from the same material. They can hardly hope for harmony as long as this holds true. Moreover, being a monopoly, the police force suffers from sluggishness; competitiveness within it must go underground, suppressed though not sublimated, awaiting opportunity. The Press has the opposite tendency, towards a neurotic hastiness characteristic of the marketplace.

An investigation which involves both analysis and dramatisation, both arrests and scoops, will combine both sets of failings. Q.E.D.

None of this was Neilson's style. He had other things to think about. And in fact he was busy elsewhere when the Press first ran foul of the police, on the 15th.

Police activity around Highley had been intense, and then suddenly attention shifted to the Swan Shopping Center in Kidderminster. Forty detectives are hard to hide in a shopping precinct, and crime squad cars make quite an impression when parked in groups with the engines running. Somebody leaked what was happening to Bill Williams, a well-established Kidderminster journalist, who rang the police station at 6 p.m. to ask for guidance.

The superintendent in charge told him he had nothing to say about the situation. Matters did not lie in his hands. He could confirm nothing, suggest nothing. He was very sorry.

So the scoop-minded Bill Williams scored a journalistic coup by putting a story over to the Birmingham Post and getting in touch with the BBC.

Until they heard the newsflash over the radio, the police at Kidderminster had no idea security had been broken. The phones started ringing at the Whittle house. The international press, which had had a field-day with the McKay case, started taking an interest.

At 10:30 the arrest-minded Detective Chief Superintendent Robert Booth bowed to the inevitable and held a press conference. The announcement he had to make was like an episode from Kojak. He regretted this. Seventeen-year-old Lesley Whittle had been kidnapped from her home in Highley while her mother slept. The ransom demand was for £50,000. She was five foot two, slim and slight, with shoulder-length mid-brown hair falling over her right eye. At the time of the disappearance she was wearing only a pair of blue slippers and a full-length pale-blue candlewick dressing-gown, with a belt, one hip pocket, and a roll collar. Otherwise she was naked, apart from a wrist-watch, a gold signet ring, and some silver jewellery made for her by her boyfriend. News of the crime had been withheld because publicity could jeopardise police arrangements for the ransom drop at Kidderminster. Booth was not too happy that someone had seen fit to release the activities police were involved with.

In fact he was absolutely bloody furious, but there was nothing he could do. He commented bitterly that they might as well pack up and go home. The whole operation, code-named with optimism Basket ("we'll soon have the bastard in the basket"), was called off for the night, and the detectives dispersed.

The breach of security did all parties a disservice. A kidnap victim has a real chance of survival if the ransom arrangements are completed within forty-eight hours. That is agreed to be the effective time limit by students of the modern kidnap, and applies irrespective of the good intentions of anyone involved.

There are three distinct phases of danger in a kidnapping—

the snatch, the drop, and the release—and only for the first (where it is necessary) is surprise possible. The picking up of the money and the setting free of the prisoner have to be negotiated, and where there is negotiation there is the possibility of being outflanked. As the hours pass a kidnapper, any kidnapper, is bound to weigh the advantages of a single act of violence against two episodes of risk.

In any case a temperament capable of an effective snatch is unlikely to solve, or even anticipate, the problems of the later stages, whose dynamics suggest a chess game instead of a commando raid. The Hoseins demonstrated this very clearly in 1969. They brought off the kidnap itself, acting almost on impulse, though admittedly they failed to get the right victim. But nothing they did thereafter showed the faintest competence. They forced Mrs. McKay to write five letters to her husband before they killed her, but couldn't even send them off in the right order to indicate she was still alive. And once they started phoning in ransom demands, they couldn't stop. Any spare moment, one of them would pop into a phone booth.

Neilson's talents were of a higher order, and he put his best into everything he did. But the difficulties he faced were no different.

Bill Williams and his informant had really shaken things up. When so much accurate information reached the Press, and was at length confirmed by the police, the clarity of the situation became blurred. From that point on the police were unable to eliminate cranks and hoaxers with any confidence. Anyone who demanded £50,000 had to be considered.

So two nights after the kidnapping Ronald Whittle had to drive from Highley to Gloucester with the white suitcases. If he didn't leave the ransom money in a park subway within ninety minutes of the phone call, he was told his sister would be killed.

Other hoaxes were easier to spot since, for no known reason, they asked for less than the full amount. One thrifty man set up a rendezvous at Paddington Station, in hopes of £2,500, and a labourer from Oldham made a play for £15,000.

All three hoaxers were arrested and convicted, but endless hours of police time were lost. The calls just kept coming, and every one had to be examined. There were several candidates who made calls on a regular basis; the police built up dossiers and analysed voiceprints.

Neilson lost by the hoaxes too; his plans depended on a stably stupid police force, and any distraction from outside weakened his control. He had no reason to thank Bill Williams for his vigilance.

Bill Williams isn't in court, looking for a final scoop to crown his career, but all the national newspapers are represented. The whole world is taking an interest.

And meanwhile negotiations are under way to publish Irene's story, My Life with the Panther, in the Sunday People. But by the time the Oxford trial is over, Irene will be in Eccleshall magistrates' court on charges of cashing stolen postal orders, and her own future will be uncertain. In court she will prefer to downplay her life with the Panther, and the sensationalised version will just have to wait.

At Kidsgrove police station Mrs. Neilson will explain that Donald has always been military minded, and she has noticed he has become fairly engrossed in camping and outdoor pursuits. He has bought a lot of camping gear in recent years. Donald can be very moody when he wants to be. He spends hours on end in his room making things and no-one is allowed in there, not ever. He goes out occasionally about six or seven o'clock in the evening and is out all night. Usually he puts his head round the door and says he is off out or going to work or something. She never bothered to see him out, so she didn't always see what he was wearing when he went. She first realised

Donald was going out stealing when she saw the postal orders in the living-room drawers in about March. She asked him where they had come from and he said, "Mind your own business." He can get violent if he is irritable. She knew better than to ask again.

So in the end the Sunday People will settle for Kathryn's side of the story instead. I am glad. I knew there was something wrong with him. I thought he was mad and I am glad they are locking him up. The fee will be £33,000, or two-thirds of the ransom demanded for Lesley Whittle.

In the dock, surrounded by policemen, Neilson keeps his face blank. But he sends definite signals by his mannerisms and his choice of clothes. He wears a dark-green single-breasted suit and a black tie, and he takes no advantage of the judge's shirt-sleeve order. The jacket remains buttoned, the tie firmly knotted. His solicitor appears every day in a shirt of a different colour, only their white collars remaining constant. But Neilson makes no attempt at variations within a basic unity; he is making a different point.

He has chosen a costume which expresses lack of choice.

Throughout the trial he takes notes. In this way he identifies himself with the jury, who must make sense of a bewildering mass of evidence and interpretation. If he just sat there and listened, he might look innocent or he might not, but he couldn't help looking passive, reconciled. As long as he writes he is the thirteenth juror, hearing things for the first time. It would be premature to act out his innocence because, as long as he keeps writing, he has yet to understand what is going on around him. It makes no difference what notes he takes; his message is the act itself of writing.

By treating the Crown case as material to be intellectually mastered, he identifies himself with the jurors; while by his rigid code of dress he differentiates himself from them. They are discharging their part of a social contract; it is appropriate that they should relax and be comfortable. Not so Neilson; no contract exists between him and the world, and by his dress he must indicate confinement.

He finds orders easier to cope with than permissions anyway. At least you know where you are.

When he comes to give evidence he tends to address himself to the judge and not his questioner. He assumes that the court is a military hierarchy in disguise, and that efficiency will be best served by his dealing direct with the commander-in-chief, disregarding the minions.

Whenever Lesley's name is mentioned in court, tears appear in Neilson's eyes though his expression doesn't change. The tears have been added from outside, or squeezed out from under a mask.

The girl gave him no trouble. He hadn't expected the girl but she co-operated from the start. He woke her up and said "No noise. I want money." She said, "It's in the bathroom." He said, "You show me." She got out of bed, she was naked. He said, "Put on some clothes," and she said, "Why?" He said, "Cover yourself," and she took a dressing-gown from the foot of the bed. Also a pair of slippers. She led towards the bathroom. The boards creaked so he took hold of her elbow and led her down the stairs. Her behaviour was never anything but correct.

When he did the job, he didn't think about people. He worked it all out and he didn't think it was a person he was getting. It was money, it was just money.

They went out of the back door through the garage and up to near a clothespost in the garden. He said again, "Where's the money? How much?" She said, "In the bathroom, in coin, two hundred pounds." It was cold and she shivered. He said, "You wait in car while I fetch money." She said, "All right."

He didn't care about the money one way or the other, but he needed to go back into the house and leave the messages.

He put sticking plaster to keep the girl's hands together, also a strip on her mouth and eyes. Then he carried her to the car which was parked in a lane down some steps. He pulled the driver's seat forward and he helped her onto the back seat beside some sponge mattresses. He said, "Don't make a sound and you OK." He closed the door then ran back to the house and left the Dymo-note on the vase in the front room, then back to the car. He sat in the driver's seat and lifted the sponge mattresses which were rolled up. He told her to lie down on the back seat and rested sponge on top so she couldn't be seen. She lay facing the back of the car.

He drove down through Highley, going to Bathpool. When he pulled onto the main road he pulled off his hood which had been on since he entered the back garden for the first time.

He drove fast down the road and after a short time the girl started struggling and making a noise. She couldn't get up because of the sponge mattresses. After they were clear of houses and street lights he pulled on the hood, stopped the car, and pulled the sponge up. She was trying to speak behind the plaster. He removed it from her mouth and said in an un-normal voice, "You have been kidnapped. Be quiet and you will not be harmed. If you do not behave I will put you in the boot. If you good, can stay where you are." She said, "Yes." He put the plaster back on her mouth, checked the heater was on warm, and drove off to Bathpool.

It was still dark but getting towards first light when they arrived. He parked close to the centre shaft and told the girl, "I will be out of the car for a couple of minutes." He started to transfer the equipment down into the shaft. He set up the lantern on a gantry, and laid out a foam-rubber sheet on the bottom landing, then a sleeping-bag on top of that.

Then he returned to the car and guided the girl to the manhole and told her to follow him down. He used a soft voice, instead of the harsh one, the voice of command, to coax her through the narrow manhole entrance and down the vertical steel ladder. The whole purpose was that there should be no hostility between the two of them. He needed her to record the tapes and it was essential that the tapes were made by her own voice, her own phrasing and showing no signs of tension or distress.

The only sign of reluctance she made was that she couldn't see where she was going, obviously, but she didn't offer any resistance. He coaxed her to the edge, and told her to bend her knees. He got her into a crouching, as it were, squatting position. He told her to put her hands on his shoulders, which was difficult for her. Again, the blindfold meant she didn't know where she was going. As she came forward, he put his hand round the back of her, underneath her legs and pulled her off balance onto himself.

There were five or six inches of water in the main tunnel. She was wearing her dressing gown and slippers and he didn't want her to get wet. He tried to carry her over his shoulder but the pipe wasn't big enough. Then he tried picking her up in his arms, as you might carry a child, but there wasn't enough room for that either. He told her her feet would have to get wet and put her down after three or four yards. He told her, "You get dry soon."

She didn't know where she was going so she had to be reassured to let her know he was on her side, as it were, even though he had kidnapped her. It was just a matter of saying, "It's OK now," in different ways to let her know she was in no danger.

The whole point of the exercise was, she would not at any time recognise him. This was the reason for the way he spoke in different voices. He said as little as possible in phrases of two or three words. He attempted to change his voice without at any time bringing harshness or hostility into it.

The girl, still blindfolded, still with her wrists tied, waded to a point where the tunnel fell away. Here she would have to skirt the hole and climb into the dry culvert to reach the bottom landing of the main shaft.

He lifted her by one hand under her bottom into the dry pipe. On the landing, he took the tape from her wrists, so she could pull off the gag and the blindfold tapes.

He confiscated her watch, and then he took off her dressing gown. There was no shame in that. He took it off her and the sleeve pulled inside out as it came off. Then he gave it back to her to dry herself with. The top part was still dry. He didn't look at her in the sense of what is meant when you say to look at somebody. He saw what there was to see, without making any intention to look. His feelings all the time were feelings of professional detachment, in the same way as a doctor accepting a patient in hospital.

She turned her back on him and got into the sleeping bag.

The Plan had been for Ronald Whittle but he couldn't complain of the girl so far. The Plan would do just as well for her anyway. From the beginning, The Plan took into consideration that the bloke would be used to living a softer, gentler, more pampered life than himself. Being further south, the climate would be warmer. It was possible, more than likely, he would be used to central heating. Therefore, the biggest fear was hypothermia or pneumonia due to sudden change in temperature, lower than he would be used to sleeping in. This was the reason for the number of sleeping-bags and survival blankets. Also for the brandy. This was intended entirely as medicinal.

He handed over the bottle wearing gloves to avoid fingerprints. She took it and said, "For me? Super." She took just three little sips, which surprised him, he thought she'd have a real drink, but she didn't. She put the top back on it and held the bottle with both hands, as you would hold a hot-water bottle, and he didn't take it from her. From the way she behaved, not drinking from it but sipping and holding it to her, he thought it was a comfort to her. He never saw her in a condition of being the worse for drink.

They did the first session of taping that morning. One of the big advantages of the drainage shaft was the noise of running water, which would drown any background noises. That would give the police next to nothing in the way of clues. They could have all the electronics in the world and still not get anywhere. There would be no sound of him on the tape.

He had a prompt script already prepared, with strips of Dymo-tape mounted on stiff card. It began: READ CARD SLOWLY AND CLEARLY INTO TAPE. Then in a different colour: SEND PERSONAL MESSAGE TELL THEM YOU OK. Then the instructions about the ransom.

The girl performed well, it was the tape recorder let him down. The quality of the recording wasn't any good. So he decided to return home to Bradford for a Sony machine with a specially-good tone. Before he left he made some chicken soup and they both had some of that. Then he tethered her to the ladder with a noose of steel wire round her neck.

The longer wire was a favour. The Plan for the bloke was to keep in one place, lying on his back with only a short wire, but there was no harm in the girl moving about a bit. She wasn't going to get up to anything.

He'd worked it all out. If he put it round the ankle, wrists, or waist it could be worked with both hands on the edge of the concrete, chafing it. It was also possible to slip it off a wrist or ankle made soft and slippery by water.

So he gave her five feet. The hands and feet were free. She could go anywhere she wanted to the limit of that distance.

When he fastened the wire she was lying in the sleeping bag with her head against the ladder. Nothing was said about what he was going to do. He padded the wire with plaster, yards and yards of it, so it wouldn't be uncomfortable. He used clips to secure the loop round her neck and then tightened them up with a spanner. The other end was secured to the ladder using similar clips.

It caused no discomfort. She made no protest and showed no signs of fear. Her conduct was never anything but correct.

Everything went well when he got back with the Sony. He'd been away a good long time, catching up on sleep and making sure the neighbours saw him, but the girl was OK.

She gave him quite a turn all the same. He must have been showering her with dirt and dust as he came down the ladder, because she was using one of the plastic sheets to shield herself. But his first thought was, this was a policeman in drag lying in wait for him. It was quite a shock, but he got over it.

He had with him some chicken legs and some fish and chips. But he knew the girl needed something to occupy her mind, so he'd picked up some stuff from the attic at home. There were two little plastic puzzles Kathryn used to like, and two brightly coloured napkins, pleasing to the eye. Also some old magazines he'd been saving to make a ransom-note out of, before he had the idea of Dymo-tape. Then there were some comforts he bought for her, some mints and some chewing-gum, The Times and some paperbacks.

She seemed quite happy, and they did the recording on the new machine. Both versions came out well; he was pleased. He taped some music for her on the other recorder, from a pocket radio he had with him. That would take her mind off things while he was away. He didn't leave the radio with her, seeing as he didn't want her hearing the news bulletins and getting

herself upset. He wouldn't be back for a while; there was lots
to do. She deserved some distraction.

The police keep Neilson under close watch throughout the
trial. He is surrounded by them. They relieve each other osten-
tatiously, as if the defendant's presence in court depends on
their unbroken concentration.

They are trying to atone for poor police performance during
the investigation, when the forces of order sinned against efficiency, against unity, and against tact. An overemphatic presence now is intended to mask past failures. The effect is one
of paradoxical weakness.

It is the same with the notice in the lobby, ABSOLUTELY NO
SMOKING PERMITTED AT ANY TIME. The redundant injunctions
only make it seem fussy and ineffectual. The police clustered
round Neilson amount to a similar message. WARNING they say,
ABSOLUTELY NO ESCAPING FROM THIS DOCK. THIS MEANS YOU.
They are a tribute to The Black Panther's notoriety, rather
than an authentic security precaution.

Various police forces are painfully conscious of a poor record on the case. The overall cost was enormous, over two
million pounds, but none of the lines of enquiry led to the
culprit. The man responsible turned out to have no criminal
record, so the intensive analysis of fingerprints, which took
priority over all other investigations and delayed them by a
matter of months, was wasted effort. Much acrimony was
generated within the force, and the shape of many careers
profoundly affected.

The McKay case had been the first of its kind in Britain
since the ransoming of Richard Coeur de Lion in 1194; the
book on the case became in effect the textbook prescribed for
the subject. The police studied it, just as Neilson did, and some
of the investigators of the McKay case saw action again in

1975. The net result of so much expertise was that both sides made advanced mistakes instead of elementary ones. Lesley Whittle was not much helped.

But at first the police altogether failed to take her disappearance seriously.

This is a problem central to the practice of kidnapping. The perfect snatch leaves no undesired traces. The kidnapper's task is then to make the victim's absence present to those left behind. He must establish clearly the difference between no message and the message No. But how is he to offer evidence of a disappearance?

Any message or tableau which the kidnapper chooses to leave behind, except perhaps his name and address, could just as easily have been left by someone faking an abduction for whatever reasons. The police, moreover, are congenitally suspicious of too much circumstantial evidence, of signs without proofs.

So for instance in the McKay case, the scene at the house looked to the police laughably like the cover of a whodunit, or an amateur production of an Agatha Christie play. There was a ball of twine, a tin of Elastoplast, and a rusty meat-cleaver. A handbag lay at the bottom of the staircase, its contents artistically strewn across the bottom five treads. An obvious set-up.

But they were no quicker to take the Whittle case seriously. Lesley's Monday clothes were where she had dropped them, but her clean ones were neatly folded on a chair. Nothing had been disturbed; even the firm's takings were still in the bathroom, waiting to be banked. Dorothy Whittle didn't even notice the Dymo-tape messages; she was looking for her daughter, and nothing else would do. The tapes were coiled among the sweets in a box of Turkish Delight, which had been placed on a large vase in front of the fireplace. Dorothy thought the little nest of red strips had something to do with Lesley's school work. It was her daughter-in-law who first examined them, later that morning.

There were four of them. They read:

NO POLICE £50 000 RANSOM BE READY TO DELIVER FIRST EVENING WAIT FOR TELEPHONE CALL AT SWAN SHOPPING CEN- TRE TELEPHONE BOX 64711 64611 63111 6PM TO 1AM IF NO CALL RETURN FOLLOWING EVENING WHEN YOU ANSWER CALL GIVE YOUR NAME ONLY AND LISTEN YOU MUST FOLLOW IN- STRUCTIONS WITHOUT ARGUMENT FROM THE TIME YOU ANSWER THE TELEPHONE YOU ARE ON A TIME LIMIT IF POLICE OR TRICKS DEATH

£50 000 ALL IN USED NOTES £25 000 £1 £25 000 £5 THERE WILL BE NO EXCHANGE ONLY AFTER £50 000 HAS BEEN CLEARED WILL VICTIM BE RELEASED

DELIVER £50 000 IN WHITE SUITCASE

SWAN SHOPPING CENTRE KIDDERMINSTER

Of course, NO POLICE wasn't a serious suggestion, it was just a convention of ransom-note composition. The note was for the police as much as anybody; he had named the sum with them in mind. The Hosein brothers had advertised their basic incompetence by demanding a million. Had shown themselves amateurs. Shown themselves wogs. Fifty thousand was a size- able chunk of the money given to the Whittles, but it was a realistic figure. It was also the sum mentioned in the McKay book as the upper limit of the European ransom demand. Figures for the States were a lot higher, but fifty thousand pounds, or its equivalent in the different currencies, was the maximum for France and Germany, and for Japan. The figure chosen was therefore a codeword aimed at the police conducting the investigation. It said: professional criminal, ambitious, hard-headed, well-read.

The message didn't get across that smoothly. There was a clear trail of muddy footprints from the soft ground outside Beech Croft, across the lounge, and up the staircase; common sense told the investigators that nothing in real life was quite that distinct. Then again, the Whittles' affluence seemed so modest that the choice of target was a complete puzzle, to anyone who had no reason to remember the distorted publicity of three years before.

The police therefore approached the ransom messages with scepticism, and extracted some satisfying contradictions from them. Like textual scholars establishing the spuriousness of a manuscript, they made much of divergences of tone and detail, form and content. Why was neither hostage nor messenger specified? Why was Dymo-tape chosen as the medium, unless to avoid using a handwriting or a typewriter which could easily be identified, perhaps by Lesley's family? YOU ARE ON A TIME LIMIT fitted in well enough with IF POLICE OR TRICKS DEATH, but where did that leave IF NO CALL RETURN FOLLOWING EVE-NING? This alternative ransom arrangement seemed remark-ably casual by contrast.

The police preferred to keep an open mind. This meant they indicated, with gentle worldliness, that young girls of a certain age do sometimes act unpredictably. It had been the same in 1969, when Mr. McKay was told that women—women of a certain age—do sometimes act unpredictably. On both occa-sions, policemen of a certain seniority utterly failed to think unpredictably. Men of a certain age, of a certain temperament, do sometimes plan the most intricate abductions.

So from the start the police were acting on two sets of premises. They would lose prestige if they showed no improve-ment on their performance in the McKay case, or alternatively if they overreacted to what might still turn out to be a hoax.

In a sense they put up a good show that first day at the

Kidderminster shopping centre. They made special arrangements to enable Ronald Whittle to withdraw the necessary money, and microfilmed every note. No single white suitcase could accommodate it all, so they used two. And they positioned a marksman under the back seat of Ronald's maroon Scimitar GTE.

But they had mislearned one of the lessons of the McKay case. The lesson was: <u>Uncontrolled publicity can damage the hostage's chances.</u> As it happened, Neilson had done his best to sidestep the whole problem, by specifying the three public telephone numbers as a guarantee of authenticity. Hoaxers in the McKay case had used the same line as the kidnappers, often in fact preventing them from getting through. Neilson made no such mistake.

The police could therefore have considered two possibilities. (1) Not all kidnappers watch television or listen to the radio. They are kidnappers first, and news-monitors second. Often they are busy, kidnapping. (2) Some kidnappers are prepared for police involvement and press coverage, and have made their plans accordingly.

A police force keeping an open mind in this way would not withdraw its forces from a rendezvous site, with four hours left to run before the deadline.

There was only one operative who wasn't told about the end of the stakeout. He was hidden inside Kidderminster telephone exchange, to tap any calls to the phone boxes.

At midnight Neilson called 64611 and let it ring for a few seconds. Two minutes later he tried 64711. Finally he rang 63111, and this time a passer-by in the deserted shopping precinct picked up the receiver. Neilson rang off without speaking.

The fiasco of Tuesday night came to light when the detective inspector from Kidderminster exchange made his report the next day. At Wednesday's press conference it was announced only that the deadline for the kidnapper's call had passed without contact. In this way the police hoped, not only to save face, but also to indicate that the phone booths were no longer any part of the investigation. Then they might have a sporting chance of completing the ransom arrangements without press interference.

But Bill Williams' run of professional luck was not yet over. He was able to find out about police plans without too much trouble, and so the evening papers that afternoon carried photos and stories clearly identifying the kiosks. The police waited the full time that night, from six to one in the morning, trying throughout to keep newsmen and crowds out of the area, but received no call from the kidnapper.

This wasn't in fact because Neilson was in any way media-shy. But he did have a lot to do, and he was interrupted.

He was laying the ransom trail. He put the first message in a phone booth on the A454 going towards Walsall. It gave directions to a booth in Coronation Avenue, on the way to Wolverhampton. The message at Coronation Avenue led to a booth on the A4123. From there the trail led to the A461 at Dudley, and to instructions taped to a street light at the Freightliner Limited terminal. The message there was CROSS ROAD AND CAR PARK GO RIGHT TO GATE NUMBER 8.

To get this far, the ransom messenger would have to double back across the M6 at Junction 10 three times. Neilson could observe any police escort and assess the chances for The Plan.

The trail was now approaching Dudley Zoo car park. The next message said INSTRUCTIONS AT END OF ROPE. The rope was a quarter-inch thick and 250 feet long. The idea was, the money suitcase to be tied to the end of the rope. Then he could haul it in without ever being seen. Escape by way of the caves and the canal tunnels.

He set everything up for the trail, then went round checking the messages were all in place before starting the whole thing off. He needed to peel back the masking tape round the message on the street light at the Freightliner terminal. As he was getting ready to adjust it, he was spotted by the overseer of the night shift.

Gerald SMITH wondered who this figure was. Perhaps a drinker from the Station Hotel, nipping down the driveway to take a leak. But the Birmingham pub bombings, high point of the IRA's campaign in England, had been only two months before, and it seemed a bad idea to take any chances.

The man was wearing a rucksack and carrying a plastic bag. He moved away from the grit bin at the depot boundary fence as Smith approached, and disappeared into the car park beside the zoo. The car park was rutted, muddy, and unlit. Smith followed him in.

Neilson stepped out from behind a lorry. "Giz a lift, mate," he said.

"A lift where?"

"Into the warehouse."

"What do you want to go in there for?"

"You find out when we get there."

The man's manner was so furtive and so strange that Smith decided to go back to his office, and phone the police. He turned round.

Neilson shot him in the buttocks. He broke into a run, and Neilson shot him in the back. Smith wheeled round and shouted a few words. A working life spent in public service on the railways left him with no natural language to express pain or frenzy. The best he could do at short notice was exasperation. "You idiot," he said. "What are you playing at?" Neilson fired four more shots in quick succession, none of which missed. The gun was now empty, and he ran.

Smith picked himself up off the ground and walked back to the terminal to inform his men. Medically, this was a mistake in itself, though an understandable one; but there was no excuse for the control with which he expressed himself when he reached the office. His brain was overruling his nervous system. "Get the police," he said. "A bloke out there just shot me. He emptied the gun at me from point-blank range."

Smith's irresponsible calm lasted all the way to the operating theatre at Dudley Guest Hospital. He asked detectives not to tell his wife what had happened till next morning. She wouldn't expect him back till then anyway, and there was no point making her lose a good night's sleep. With this final inversion of priorities, Smith was wheeled away for the first of many operations.

The police had no reason to link the Dudley shooting with any other crime, but they had within reach a huge body of evidence which would establish the connections. This was the dark green Morris 1300 used in the kidnap, now parked opposite the Midland Red bus garage in Dudley. Standard police procedure demanded the checking of every car parked within a one-mile radius of the shooting, but somehow the stolen Morris, with its false number plates and clumsily altered road fund license, escaped detection. The police national computer was used to analyse the data, but came up with nothing useful.

Neilson was far too canny to come anywhere near the car again, though he had left damaging traces in it: samples of his characteristic handwriting, with its plentiful full stops and distinctive letter A. He took it for granted the car was under surveillance, and he knew better than to walk into a police trap. But the police weren't being canny at all.

The jury sits and sweats. Obediently the jury members shuffle through their folders, searching out the page numbers as directed. The barristers make pointed pauses in their addresses to make sure that the jurors are looking at the right place.

Expectations of the jury are not high, however. In theory they are sovereign, in practice, sheep.

This isn't an unsatisfactory situation. The big potential drawback of holding the trial in Oxford lay in the composition of the jury. There was a real danger that members of the academic community might be empanelled. They are poorly suited to jury service. Twelve good men and true is the system's description of itself, but good men and thick would define things more clearly. Too much independence, too much originality in any one juror, could upset the balance of forces on which the system depends. The trial would become a nightmare, for instance, if the jury included two rival criminology dons, writers of detective novels in their spare time. Utterly sure of their grasp of the case, they would seek to apply their theories of motivation and responsibility, and pass pert little notes to witnesses, asking was the remaining muffin tested for fingerprints?

Nothing of the sort occurred. The jurors make no excessive individual contribution to the running of the case; they are exemplary in their willingness to follow.

But it isn't easy keeping track of the paperwork. The dossiers in front of them contain statements, photographs, and endless lists of exhibits. The colour values of the police photographs, in which blood shows up as brown, compare unfavourably with Neilson's photo of Irene playing dead, which is included in the folders. The ketchup stains admirably attract the eye.

Prominent among the documents in their folders are the statements made by Neilson after his arrest. Their flatness of tone conceals an extraordinarily structured language. Naked except for a blanket, and with his hands handcuffed behind his back, Neilson nevertheless worked harder in Kidsgrove police station than he had ever worked in his life. He allowed questions to remain unanswered for minutes on end, and when they asked him why he was taking so much time:

"I am thinking, sir.

"I have to think carefully.

"I need time to think," he said.

He was thinking all right. In those hours he was constructing for himself a grammar of innocence. He needed to articulate the facts without losing his sense of himself. He needed to accommodate the police version of all that had happened, within a larger framework. His memories existed in rough cut; here they received their final editing.

For years he had been thinking his own thoughts and evolving his own values without reference to anyone else. Even if Irene and Kathryn felt the force of his actions, they knew nothing of his thoughts. But now he had to engage with a public language at last, or with an authoritative private one.

It was a tremendous effort. But no-one ever suggested he was a bad joiner. He could make things fit, and he could make them hold together.

The casualties of this language, the meanings which could not be expressed by it, were the sentences police and prosecution wanted to hear, guilty sentences like, "I threatened her with the gun," "I deliberately pulled the trigger," "he was blocking my way so I shot him."

None of these sentences survived translation. Action was divided into two parts separated by a long interval: The Plan and its execution. The Plan excluded violence and worked towards the greatest good of the greatest number. It was therefore innocent. But any unforeseen element was an accident, and nobody's fault.

He used a single past tense, with no imperfect or pluperfect to separate out levels of distance in time. Whenever he said, "the intention was" (or more rarely, "I meant"), he was talking about The Plan, which preceded the raids by weeks or months. And when he was out on a job he wasn't a choosing being. He had the normal reactions, but he wasn't deciding things.

By limiting his definition of volition, he disposed of the idea of guilty intention on which criminal law is based.

Example: "I threatened her with the gun" became "the gun was a threat." In this way he disclaimed any direct transmission of fear. If the girl chose to be frightened, that was her business. Looked at in the right way, the gun and the costume were reassuring. A sawn-off shotgun meant "professional criminal," it was the tool for the job, it looked as if it meant business; it was the weapon understood by everyone, and it said I know what I'm doing. The hood and the costume made him unrecognisable, so they were saying You can't identify me so there's no reason why I should hurt you. Properly understood, his appearance was more a comfort than anything else.

The gun had inverted commas round it; it was a cue for a particular type of behaviour. It wasn't a gun, the way a gun in a war is a gun. He never used violence.

The hood distinguished sharply between obsessive planner and ritual functionary. From the moment he put it on, he was a lord of misrule, rather than a citizen transgressing. There was exactly as much human-being left in him as there is in a commando on a raid, every reflex at the service of an idea.

If an American judge, who asserts his authority with a gavel, is armed then so was he. In the gun he had a symbolic weapon. It could kill, just as the judge could rise from the judgement-seat and lash out murderously with his ritual hammer. But the essential function of both tools was to focus attention by their simple presence, or by sounding a warning.

The times the gun went off, it had been misunderstood. The postmasters were killed by a rogue element of criminal language.

He was taking so long addressing himself to the questions that they started doing some prompting.

Q: Have you had time to think?

A: Yes sir, I think so.

Twenty-five minutes of silence.

For a good long while he assumed a middle-European accent and a clipped delivery, and they asked if he was Welsh. Then the questions got properly under way.

Q: (fingering an artist's impression of The Black Panther) A man wearing a hood is wanted for some serious offenses in various parts of the country. I suspect you are that man.

Five minutes.

A: Not true. I no shoot anybody (= shooting anything but a warning shot has never been part of The Plan).

Q: You would have used the shotgun on anyone who caught you, wouldn't you? You're a one-man combat unit, aren't you?

Seven minutes.

A: Would shoot dog but no policeman. I no Black Panther (who is an invention of the Press). When (") Black Panther (") work, he shoot to kill. (There's no such person).

Q: Do you know Highley? Are you familiar with Bathpool Park? Are you the man responsible for the kidnapping and murder of Lesley Whittle?

Eleven minutes.

A: No, sir. Not me. Not murder the young girl (= her death was accidental). I know you got job to do. I realise that, but it is too distressing.

Q: You had an accomplice, didn't you?

Twenty-two minutes.

A: I didn't murder her. I didn't even know who I was going to get from the house. People believe all the lies about this Black Panther. The papers don't tell the truth. The Black Panther, so called, they tell lies about him. I read them. He is not like they say. I want to tell you the truth. I do not tell you lies like the newspapers. Can you protect my wife and daughter if I make a statement? I want to make a statement. I want everybody to know the truth. The girl need not have died if the money had been paid.

He retrieved himself from this outburst when it came to making a statement. He spent nearly nine hours dictating his version of what passed between him and Lesley Whittle, and that still left Harrogate, Accrington, Langley, and Dudley to be accounted for. He stopped to consider every word, deleting items and initialling alterations, reading through some passages as many as six times.

This was wasted effort as far as the jurors are concerned; it's just one document among the many. At first sight, the statements are too strange to be understood, but after a few days they become too familiar to be recognised.

The sweating jurors will take with them when they retire to consider their verdicts the first of the ransom tapes, discovered at long last in the Morris 1300 at Dudley. But even that can produce no epiphany of horror, however many times it is played. Lesley's voice is even and well-modulated; in spite of its hollowness, the recording quality suggests a sitting-room rather than a dungeon. She enunciates the instructions so calmly that she makes wanting to be retrieved from a drainage shaft sound like a mild domestic request.

She is sixty feet below ground, tethered round the neck, naked inside a sleeping-bag. It is three years since her father died. The script she must read is taped to the stomach of the man who has kidnapped her; he shines his torch on it. Her brother Ronald is fourteen years older than she is, and if he tells her something it's because he knows best. The man nods. He has spoken only a few words, but he has told her it will be all right. She starts to speak.

"Go to the M6 north to Junction 10 and then onto the A454 towards Walsall. Instructions are taped under the shelf in the telephone box. Please mum . . .

"There's no need to worry, mum. I'm okay. I got a bit wet but I'm quite dry now. I'm being treated very well. OK?"

The jurors have so much to think about. They must pay

attention to their folders, and the barristers, and the witnesses, and still keep a weather eye out for the judge.

From the start the judge has subjected the jury to obedience training. He bows to them each time the court reassembles, and after a few false starts they have learned to bow back again in approximate unison. They are eager to express their appreciation of the judge's attention; they incline their heads winningly, as if acknowledging an important personage at a social occasion. His overpowering deference has tamed them utterly.

The judge asks tenderly after their concentration whenever he sees a juror's mouth drop open. This is a risky procedure, since it tends to reveal unsuspected sleepers, who sit suddenly upright and announce that No, they are one-hundred-per-cent alert. The judge then suggests a brief adjournment.

The two advocates are careful to cultivate opposite styles. They have everything in common in terms of background and prospects, education and opinions; they are well known to each other socially. But it is a part of their job which has by now become automatic, to impersonate opposing and embattled principles. Their smooth alternation, their ability to anticipate each other's moves, depends on a considerable familiarity; from time to time their similarity becomes evident, and an uncalled-for amity shows through. When a defense counsel appears more intimate with his opponent than his client, an obscure restlessness is felt by the spectators.

In this case Mr. Philip Cox represents the Crown; his learned friend Mr. Gilbert Gray appears for the defense.

In spite of the heat Mr. Cox is impeccably turned out, and carries himself with conspicuous ease of manner. His wig sits as lightly and as naturally on his head as if it grew there. His gown follows his unemphatic gestures; it endorses his poses with a sober rustling. The starched bands at his neck can hardly be comfortable, but no undue colour shows in his face.

His control of himself is somehow tied in with his command of the case, and his conviction of the rightness of every connection he makes. How could he be asking for the verdict of Guilty if there remained for him the slightest particle of doubt?

His posture asserts that for him there exist no intermediate states; with anything less than absolute certainty, he could not function at all. His junior prepares references and administers the paperwork with the same seamless calm. If at any time Mr. Cox half-turns, in need of a corroborating detail, the relevant note is awaiting his hand.

With their gestures they enact the thoroughness and inevitability of their version of the facts; self-possession is nine parts of their case.

Mr. Gray, by contrast, is bothered and almost distracted. He is clearly uncomfortable in judicial dress; the placement of his wig never satisfies him for more than seconds at a time. More than once his junior has to attract his attention in mid-sentence, and a tiny conference must be carried on in whispers before the case can proceed. His dress verges on the sloppy, his gown hangs low and lopsided from his shoulders. His gestures are awkward; they seem hampered if anything by the heavy material.

Mr. Gray's bearing expresses mistrust of a superficial order. Human passions and disorders are poorly served by the rigours of the law, which reduces life in all its plurality to a verdict of Yes or No. It's not that he's being difficult; he would accept Mr. Cox's view of the case if he could. But there is much to be said on both sides of the question, on every side of every question. He never ceases to adjust his dress, as if the reason-able doubt of which he seeks to convince the jury were roving as an itch beneath wig and gown.

In his advocacy Mr. Cox aims at a classicism in which simple declarative sentences put all the relevant information in order. Complex syntax would be a mistake; the jury might suspect, however dimly, that discrepancies were being hidden, that a subordinate clause was tidying an unruly fact out of sight, while seeming to account for it. He seeks to maintain a single consistent tone; he excludes even appeals to conventional feeling until the closing passages of his final speech.

Mr. Gray by contrast is all for the romantic approach. He responds to Mr. Cox's steady line with an explosion of subversive suggestions, only one of which need find its target for his efforts to succeed. His language is full of allusions, extravagant comparisons, and tricks of speech; the grammatical thrust of his sentences is dissipated among his many parenthetical remarks. Only rarely does he contest the facts; but he gives himself a free hand in the interpretation department.

He feels free to use words which the jury will find hard to understand, Latinisms and the like; reasonable doubt of any kind is to be welcomed, even doubt on the part of the jury about the defendant's being adequately represented.

He persists in his extravagance when addressing the judge.

MR. GRAY: A further trial is unnecessary and an act of otiose supererogation. . . . It is not a question of this man with the feline appellation having nine lives, each one of which has to be taken from him. Saturation bombing is not a part of English jurisprudence and should be shunned.

Mr. Gray isn't afraid to mix his tones and to introduce various elements of comedy into his addresses. He specialises in an exasperated sarcasm.

A jury which has been coaxed into laughter at the defendant's expense will be that much less likely to convict. A murder trial is after all a serious business, from which laughter is banished as a matter of course; once a juror has laughed, he is inevitably alienated from the ritual role that he is being called on to play. A tonal doubt has been created. There is also, for an English jury, a feeling that a man who has first been laughed at, and then convicted, has been exposed to a double jeopardy. It seems fair to send a wrongdoer to the stocks to be derided, or to a prison to be confined, but not to strip him of dignity and liberty, one after the other.

Mr. Gray is not, therefore, merely amusing himself with his sallies.

MR. GRAY: You have heard much, members of the jury, about Mr. Neilson, and the Black Panther; but you may, when you have heard of this man's pathetic attempts to "make it big," think rather of the Pink Panther and Mr. Peter Sellers.

Mr. Gray's argument may be represented in diagram so:

(This man), this lance corporal who fancied himself as a general, a planner of campaigns, with logistics and supplies, this frustrated man of modest military rank, this Walter Mitty asserting himself in a world of his own invention, (put himself), always with his absurd plans ready for the tactical withdrawal or strategic abandonment of the entire scheme, (in a series of positions) designed to give full rein to his fantasies of military supremacy (in which accidents had fatal consequences for these unfortunate people) and to compensate for the grotesque lack in his character of any ability to live in the world as it is.

This line of defense seems enormously unwelcome to Neilson, who stiffens his posture still further and fixes his representative throughout with a stare of rage.

The clerk of the court receives numbered and labelled exhibits from the police and hands them to jurors and witnesses. But how is he to carry himself? Is he an agent of impartial analysis, or is he a momentary focus of theatre? He resolves the tension between his senses of drama and fair play by handling every object without exception, as if it were stained with heart's blood.

The witnesses take their places in the stand and falter their way through the oath, all except the policemen and expert witnesses, who rattle off the petitions like grace before food and curb their impatience with the clerk's unnecessary prompting.

Extensive provisions have been made for the faithful of various sorts, for whom an oath sworn on the Bible would not amount to a spiritual imperative. Selected holy books can therefore be substituted for it, and the associated scraps of ritual can briefly be accommodated in the court of the Queen's Justice. Sikhs wishing to swear on the Granth, for instance, are obliged to wash feet and hands before and after approaching their sacred text, which is protected from profanation by layers of white cloth. A similar latitude is granted to some Oriental sects, which dispense with a book and use an egg or a saucer instead; the witness to be sworn takes the object in his hands, and swears as he breaks it that he desires no other fate for his soul, if he lie.

Proformas for all these variations are at the clerk's disposal, and a witness dissatisfied with all these options can eliminate holy book or symbolic object altogether, and simply affirm. The law wishes only for the strongest commitment of which each individual is capable. But all these witnesses choose the conventional bond, though they act as if they have never seen a bible before, and in several cases seem unwilling to touch it.

In strong contrast are the policemen, who are much at home with the procedure, and grasp the book like people seeking to impress with their firmness of handshake.

The widows, Mrs. Skepper, Mrs. Astin, Mrs. Grayland, keep their voices down to a whisper and have to be told from time to time to speak up. The judge makes it his special concern to put them at their ease, telling them to take as much time as they want. But their sole priority is getting it over with, and if they slow down it is only from fear of disobeying him. In any case, they are caught in a crossfire of charisma, with the judge on their left speaking words of comfort while Neilson on their right gives the look of power everything he's got. Mrs. Grayland, who was not recognised by the local policeman who discovered her, with no detectable pulse or blood-pressure, under a pile of boxes, has made a remarkable recovery but is still the most subdued of the three. A woman detective sits by her to give moral support. She solves the problem of having two authorities competing for her attention by looking straight ahead of her, though not at the jury either, and reciting her evidence in a scarcely audible voice. She makes no attempt at greater volume even when coaxed with gentle persistence by the judge, whose elevation above the court makes his obligingness suspect.

Ronald Whittle is stiff and nervous from the word go. At the beginning of the case he was perceived by the public as shifty, perhaps even the engineer of the kidnap, greedy (obviously) for his sister's inheritance as well as his own. In consequence he has come to look harassed and untrustworthy.

A recurring rumour at the time of the kidnap suggested that he wasn't doing all he could for the poor girl, for reasons of his own. The crucial fact unknown to outsiders was that he was pretending to act independently, as demanded by the ransom notes, while all the time working closely with the police. Having to say one thing and do another, to accept advice from the police and all the time await instructions from the kidnapper, proved an absurd load to carry, besides being irrelevant to the realities of the case.

Even now he looks exhausted. But what really wore him out was the night of 16 January 1975, the third day of Lesley's disappearance.

Neilson's persistence was heroic. Two attempts at a ransom run had fallen through, but still he didn't give up on his project. He kept an unstable situation steady by sheer force of will, and if Lesley Whittle's lifespan as a kidnap hostage was longer than the average, the credit must go to him.

The call was taken by the manager of the Whittle depot at Highley. The family had asked him if he minded having their line plugged through to his extension. He heard the pay-tone bleeps of a public callbox and then Lesley's voice. He tried to interrupt, to say <u>where are you</u> and <u>are you all right</u>, but she went right on talking, calm as anything, and of course he realised it was a recording. The message was delivered three times.

"Please mum, you are to go to Kidsgrove post-office telephone box. The instructions are inside, behind the backboard. I'm okay. But there's to be no police and no tricks, OK? Please mum . . ."

The time was 11:30 p.m. The depot manager rang Ronald to tell him it was Lesley this time all right. Ronald rang the Bridgnorth incident room, and they told him to stay where he was.

While he was waiting he looked up Kidsgrove on a map. When midnight passed without word from Bridgnorth, he rang them up again. This time they said he should come to Bridgnorth for a briefing.

At the police station he waited fifteen minutes in an office while the police made their preparations. The ransom money was transferred to his car.

Ronald was fitted out with one-way radios transmitting on the police surveillance frequency, one in the car, one in his jacket pocket worked by a throat microphone. There was no way for the police to communicate with him. He was given instructions on the use of the radios, and told that a distress call would bring help within two minutes.

By the time he left Bridgnorth for the ransom run proper,

it was 1:30, about the time a kidnapper would be expecting him to make contact. And in fact an advance party of West Mercia and Scotland Yard police was already at Kidsgrove, planning strategy on-the-spot. They set up a mobile control van with a self-contained communications network high up on Mow Cop, about six miles from Kidsgrove, so as to avoid radio blind spots. But finding a good home for the hardware didn't compensate for slowing down the ransom messenger.

A relaxed, mature kidnapper would know better than to worry. But a less perfectly adjusted criminal, particularly one who had included a passage about BEING ON A TIME LIMIT FROM THE MOMENT YOU ANSWER THE TELEPHONE in his ransom note, might do anything.

Twice Ronald Whittle missed turnings for Kidsgrove and lost his way. It was almost 3 a.m. before he reached the phone box. He followed police instructions and reported every step he took to the squad in the van on Mow Cop.

"I am searching behind the backboard of the kiosk.

"There is nothing.

"I am searching the ledges. . . .

"Now I am examining the floor. . . .

"There is nothing here.

"I can't be in the right phone box.

"I am leaving the kiosk. There must be another phone box nearby."

But there wasn't, so he went back for another search.

.   .   .

"I am having a cigarette.

"There's just nothing here.

"I'm going to ring Hodge, that's all I can do."

Hodge was the Assistant Chief Constable of West Mercia, and Ronald had been given the number for use in emergency.

Hodge told him to stay in the phone box, to keep searching, and to ring again in fifteen minutes.

After fifteen minutes Hodge told him to search the box again.

This time Ronald seemed to get farther behind the backboard and he thought his fingertips brushed something.

Even after that, it took him twenty minutes to retrieve the message. It read:

GO TO THE END OF THE ROAD AND TURN INTO BOAT HORSE LANE GO TO THE TOP OF THE LANE AND TURN INTO NO ENTRY GO TO THE WALL AND FLASH LIGHTS LOOK FOR TORCH LIGHT RUN TO TORCH FURTHER INSTRUCTIONS ON TORCH THEN GO HOME AND WAIT FOR TELEPHONE.

The instructions took Ronald into Bathpool Park. There was ground fog in patches and very little moon. The Park is an area of former mine workings and waste tips, with landscaped hillocks and an artificial ski-slope to transform it into a beauty spot and amenity area. There is a reservoir at one end and a main railway line along one of its edges. No houses overlook it.

Without the benefit of military training and knowledge of the terrain, Ronald had no chance of finding the WALL mentioned in the instructions. It was only a low parapet really, marking the point where the path overlooks the mouth of the railway tunnel. Instead of stopping at the invisible nexus represented by the WALL, Ronald drove slowly on down the track.

He stopped at the far end of the park and flashed his lights, and spent about half an hour patrolling back and forth.

He flashed his lights continually, but there was no answer. Eventually he got out of the car and shouted.

"Hello, This is Ron Whittle, Can you hear me, Is anyone there?"

But that did no good either. By now the rendezvous had been missed by hours and not by minutes.

But why had the strip of tape in the phone box been so hard to reach? It wasn't in Neilson's interests, or even in character, to foul up his own ransom trail. A policeman of the advance party, though, checking that the message was there, could have pushed it out of reach when replacing it. Neilson didn't do anything wrong except kill people and steal them from their homes; the police didn't do anything right except mean well and hope for the best.

This is only one of the embarrassing doubts which Detective Chief Superintendent Robert Booth must try to disperse when he comes to testify. His reputation before the Whittle case was matchless, but now it is in shreds. He is widely thought to have let a difficult case obsess him and impair his judgement. Colleagues from other forces snub him as he waits outside the courtroom for his turn in the witness-box. There are clear signs of bitterness and hurt visible, as he sits there, in his heavy bland public-official's face. In only a week he will be back in uniform as head of the Malvern division after twenty-five years in the CID. His Chief Constable will describe the move as a routine cross-posting.

Bathpool Park was the source of most of the trouble. After the failure of the rendezvous, a search of the most thorough kind was called for, but no such thing took place.

Booth's understanding was that the Yard men would take charge of the search, in fact that all other personnel were to be excluded from the operation. But the officers loaned by the

Yard were specialists in surveillance work who felt they would be wasted on a routine search. The Yard left that side of things to West Mercia. The result was a cursory search which revealed nothing.

Only after weeks without new information was a proper house-to-house search of the area arranged; appeals for information were at last made to the public. This in turn offended the local police; Bathpool Park lay in Staffordshire's jurisdiction, but no-one there knew anything about the failed ransom run till they turned on the TV and found it was public knowledge.

Meanwhile clues from the Park started turning up. Two schoolboys gave in a hand-lantern torch, which had been wedged in a flood-water spillway. They remembered there had been a strip of tape attached, but they had thrown it away. Two other schoolboys handed in the tape, reading DROP SUITCASE IN HOLE, which they had found entangled in a sapling. A schoolgirl out riding two days after the ransom run had spotted some odds and ends, and led police to a pair of binoculars, an anorak, a hammer, and a split holdall. Another Kidsgrove girl had found a stopwatch near Peacocks Hay Road. An additional pair of schoolboys brought in two vacuum flasks, a black plastic mac, and two sugar buns in a plastic bag. They had made these finds on January 17, when the buns were still quite soft to the squeeze. The flasks had held soup but they had poured that away.

As late as April 8 a tangle of crumpled cassette tape with Lesley's Kidsgrove message turned up, and the schoolboy responsible for finding it surprised everyone by stumbling across a discarded tape-recorder two days later.

But by that time the drainage complex had been explored at last, and the world's attention had shifted once and for all to the levels beneath the Park. On March 6 a Staffordshire officer entered the complex at the point where the DROP SUIT-

CASE INTO HOLE torch had been left. Below, he found a Dymo-tape machine and a roll of Elastoplast. At the second level of the main shaft he found a tape-recorder and a Winfield Reporter's Notebook, in the mouth of a dry culvert. With the help of his torch he could also see a full-length pale blue candlewick dressing-gown with a tie belt, one hip pocket, and a roll collar, draped from a platform. A girl's naked body was hanging next to it. The wire around her neck was snagged on a projecting iron stanchion, and her toes were only six inches from the bottom of the tunnel.

Lesley Whittle had been missing for almost two months, and her family had for some time been contemplating the probability of her death. But Det. Ch. Supt. Booth couldn't control his emotions when he came to announce the news to a press conference. "Staffordshire have got our body," he said.

The news meant that his involvement in the case would be much restricted. Now that Staffordshire had got West Mercia's body, Staffordshire and Scotland Yard would divide the investigation between them, and West Mercia would only be left with the kidnapping aspect.

Booth was still so visibly upset at Lesley's funeral that the vicar, the Revd. John Britain, addressed words of comfort to him. "In the early days of this enquiry," he stated in the course of his address, "Mr. Booth said: 'In my book she is still alive.' May I say, sir, now, don't cross that out of your book, for in my Book Lesley is still alive, even though her mortal remains are here."

The rest of the vicar's speech offered less consolation to the investigators. It was the saddest day in the history of Highley. All those present were well aware of the tragic circumstance that had led to the sad occasion, to the brutal and untimely death of a lovely and inoffensive girl. What had happened to their sister and child, Lesley, reminded them forcibly of the fact that they were living in an age when demon possession was a reality. What individual could have put his hand to such atrocities, as the person responsible had done and who was possessed by the Devil? It was indeed the work of the Devil. He had indeed laid his hand on their village.

The man chosen by the Yard to take charge and exorcise the demon of failure was Commander John Morrison. His position as head of the Murder Squad testified to concern in high police places for the sensitiveness of a case already marked by poor organisation and personality clashes. He had a reputation for toughness and diplomacy.

But Booth wasn't finished yet. He could still hold press conferences every bit as well as Staffordshire could, and he could drop bombshells of his own. One day, for instance, he announced that the culprit would be arrested within the next twenty-four hours, at a stage when the Staffordshire faction was reporting the most moderate progress. Booth's gamble was based on the assumption that only a few people had taken part in the construction of the drainage complex, and that no-one else could have come across it. All the same, his credibility lasted until the time limit ran out without the promised arrest. Even then, Booth tried to hold on to original documents requested by the Yard for its investigation, but by this time opposition to him was strong. He tried to defy a ban on his divisive press conferences, but was reduced to silence at last when the chief constables united against him.

Here in court Booth does his best to expound his view of the case, but he is not by now a popular man, and the judge rebukes him for attacking his colleagues under the cloak of absolute privilege enjoyed by witnesses in legal proceedings.

Very much more popular as witnesses are Police Constables White and McKenzie, who came across Neilson quite by chance on their beat in Mansfield Woodhouse, and eventually effected his arrest.

The two were patrolling in their Panda car when they spotted an unfamiliar figure.

P.C. WHITE: Good evening, sir. At this time of night we always check out strangers. Would you mind telling us your name, address, and where you have been?

NEILSON: (inaudible mumble).

P.C. MCKENZIE: Can we have your name, date and place of birth, please?

NEILSON: I'm John Moxon. I was born at Chapel-en-le-Frith on the thirtieth of January 1937.

WHITE: What are you doing?

NEILSON: I'm a lorry driver. I've just finished work.

When the policeman looked up from jotting down his details, Mr. Moxon was pointing a gun.

NEILSON: Don't move.

The climax of the incident came when members of the public waiting in a queue at the Junction Chippy heard a shout from the street outside: "Help me for God's sake he's got a gun."

Two men ran to help with hardly a moment's hesitation, though they were at the very front of the queue; one of them even knew a little karate. Taking a good look at Neilson's jacket to make sure he had the right man, he administered a disabling blow to the side of the neck, gashing his little finger but quieting Neilson considerably.

The four heroes of the arrest offer a more pleasing picture of police-public co-operation than the investigation as a whole ever did. Even if it was chance that brought Neilson their way, they got the right man, and without ransom notes, journalists, self-contained communications networks, and professional jealousies, they managed pretty well. It isn't surprising that so much celebratory stress is placed on these four. The civilians are awarded £250 apiece, while the policemen are promoted and receive the Queen's Medal for Gallantry. All four are presented with gold watches, and the general air of congratulation goes some way towards obscuring the stark failures of the past.

By the time he comes to give evidence, it isn't any longer a question of Neilson's being acquitted. The issue is whether he will be able to hold on to his idea of himself under cross-examination. Will he be strong enough to resist the definition of him given by Mr. Cox?

Maintaining a story under cross-examination is very different from dictating one in a police station; there is no reading back six times, no deleting, no altering. There is only the witness, with his vast half-buried need to conform, and the man with the professional tools to uncover the Yes beneath the No.

The moment Neilson finishes an answer, Mr. Cox has another question ready. Neilson is prevented from establishing his own tempo. He pauses after each question to recast it mentally in his own terms; but it is the hardest thing in the world to keep a vision alive, even a corrupt one, in circumstances like these.

Sometimes Neilson simply refuses to enter into a dialogue.

MR. COX: If the gun was only the tool for the job, why did you fit it with a silencer?

Why was that necessary?

Because you were perfectly prepared to fire that gun, weren't you?

Not just a warning shot, of course. You had no objection to shooting someone if it helped you to get away, did you?

I suggest to you that your plans always included the possibility of killing.

Am I not right?

.   .   .

Neilson chooses to make no contribution to this line of argument. At another stage he fights for agonised seconds against a sudden military-style order.

MR. COX: Very well, Mr. Neilson. If your hood was not a means of terrorising your victim, you will have no objection to putting it on. (Snapping harshly) <u>Put it on. Show the jury what you looked like to this young girl.</u>

Neilson has the hood in his hands. He raises it to shoulder-level and beyond, casting desperate glances at his counsel.

MR. GRAY: That is a most improper suggestion.

Neilson freezes. The judge decides that the suggestion is proper but not in any way binding, and Neilson returns the hood to the clerk of the court without trying it on. But perhaps Mr. Cox has achieved as much as he expected.

Mr. Gray's use of cross-examination technique is inevitably different. He must give the impression of asking beady-eyed questions, do-you-really-expect-me-to-believe-that questions, without actually gathering new information. He is experienced enough as an advocate to sense latent masses of unwelcome testimony in some of the witnesses. He must force them to leave this unexpressed, by phrasing his questions with great care and warning them with great emphasis against the sin of irrelevance.

Mrs. Grayland, for instance, as the most spectacularly widowed and damaged witness, clearly has it in her to reduce the court to a hush of pathos. The only course open to Mr. Gray is to defuse Mr. Grayland's death by sanctifying it, turning it into the tragic but characteristic end of a self-sacrificing life. What widow will be able to resist a line of argument which makes so much of the courage of the deceased?

Mrs. Grayland for one. She hasn't sufficiently recovered from her injuries to be manipulated in the recognised ways. She isn't well enough to respond correctly to the treatment.

MR. GRAY: (soft, sympathetic) If anyone tried to get into the post office, your husband would have put up a resistance?

MRS. GRAYLAND: (doing her best) I suppose he would have tried.

MR. GRAY: (calculated risk) There are those who would say to an intruder "Here, take the lot."

MRS. GRAYLAND: (unable to oblige) We always said that if anyone broke in, our lives were more precious than the money. I would have been prepared to hand it over. But we were not even given that chance.

The court is reduced to a hush of pathos, and Mr. Gray blames himself. But it could happen to anybody.

In his dealings with his client, Mr. Gray can only prepare Neilson by taking him stage by stage through his evidence, giving him a rehearsal of the grilling which awaits him; a homeopathic dose of fierceness. Some crucial passages of the kidnap statement are worryingly thin, and Neilson will need a lot of help if he is to defend them.

His statement about the death itself is short on depth and detail. Neilson was waiting for the arrival of the ransom messenger. The police were setting up the equipment on Mow Cop. A helicopter passed overhead, convincing Neilson that a police trap was in operation, and that the ransom money would not in fact be handed over. He entered the shaft.

NEILSON: As I came out of the short tunnel on to the platform, the girl moved to her right to allow me on to the platform beside her. As I stood on the platform, she went over the side and was suspended from the wire I had placed there earlier to prevent her leaving the tunnel. I moved to the side of the platform that she had gone over. Her head was below the level of the platform. I saw her face; her eyes seemed to be half closed and stopped moving. I froze, then panicked. The next thing I remember is shoving the cover up to get out.

. . .

The wire caused sudden high pressure in the carotid artery. The vagus nerve signalled for the pressure to be lowered. The brain obliged by slowing the heart, and then brought it to a standstill when that made things no better. Heart massage, within a minute or two, would have brought her back.

Now Mr. Gray coaches Neilson through his version, hoping for something unshakeable.

NEILSON: I descended the ladder about three rungs at a time. The time to stop, the time to rest, was after I got to the bottom of the ladder. As I came out of the dry culvert I looked down and saw she was there in the normal position. At a glance down I saw she started to move, as she normally did, to allow me to get on to the platform beside her. She moved away from the ladder and to her right. As I took my foot off the ladder and turned to face the front, I looked round and she went over. The lantern was still lit and I grabbed this and stepped across the other side of the landing and put my foot down on the concrete ledge and went down, as it were, into a crouching position in front of her. I held my left hand down and towards her with the intention of pulling her back up. Her head was lower than the gantry and she was hanging, as it were, from underneath. There was some movement when I first got down there. Her right hand was stretched out behind her, moving. Her other arm was bent at the elbow. Her fists were clenched. There was nothing to grab hold of. The torch was pointing into her face. Her eyes flickered and stopped. Everything stopped. There was no movement. It was then I realised she was dead. This stopped me as it were, dead in my tracks. She was dead. There was absolutely nothing I could do. And I am telling this court that from the time I stepped on to the landing to her being dead would be somewhere in the region of three to four seconds. As far as I am concerned she died in those four seconds. She was dead before I left her and I say, through being there and seeing it, she positively didn't take minutes as has been said by forensic doctors. She did NOT take minutes to die. She was dead in seconds. She was dead before I left.

MR. GRAY: Can you define your attitude towards her death?

NEILSON: She was dead before I left her and I do not hold myself responsible for her death. It was not my doing.

Mr. Cox waits for several long moments before he rises.

MR. COX: You had planned her death hadn't you?

NEILSON: No, sir, at no point whatsoever.

MR. COX: She did die and you were not arrested until December, eleven months later?

NEILSON: Agreed.

MR. COX: Her body was found only two months later?

NEILSON: Only? It should have been found next morning.

MR. COX: It is not part of the court's duty to investigate police procedures.

NEILSON: That's a pity.

MR. COX: Because Lesley Whittle died, your planning had been so complete that you nearly got away scot-free?

NEILSON: I did get away scot-free.

MR. COX: I suppose you are proud of that?

NEILSON: I am proud of the fact that The Plan worked, my Lord. I am talking about the entirety of The Plan, not in any way the death. That was not part of The Plan.

MR. COX: But despite all the careful preparation of The Plan, it failed because you blundered. You left a writing-pad in the shaft with a fingerprint on it.

NEILSON: That wasn't in the shaft, that was in the car. That was never found in the shaft.

MR. COX: You see, Mr. Neilson, you cannot bear the thought of having slipped up, can you?

NEILSON: That is not so. I am not going to say this was in the drainage place and then you bring twenty witnesses to say this was in the bloody car.

MR. COX: You slipped up again with the hood. You allowed Lesley to see your face.

NEILSON: No.

MR. COX: If she had seen your face, she was a person who was able to recognise you on a subsequent occasion, wasn't she?

NEILSON: Yes.

MR. COX: And if that happened, you couldn't allow her to live, could you?

NEILSON: I would have had to . . .

MR. COX: You would have had to kill her, wouldn't you? Let me remind you of what you told the jury. You had been talking about coming down the ladder and my learned friend, Mr. Gray, asked you, "Did you say anything to indicate your alarm?" to which you replied, "As I said before, there must have been something in my face, something in my expression." Mr. Gray then said, "Did you have a hood on at this time?" You changed your story and then replied, "It must have been something in my manner."

NEILSON: She saw the eyes which were behind the mask. The expression of concern could be seen in the eyes through the mask. When I went down and saw the polythene sheet which was strange to me, I did not know whether it was her under the sheet or whether it was a policeman in drag.

MR. COX: I suggest to you that in that piece of evidence, you told the truth: that you were down the shaft with this girl without your mask?

NEILSON: Not at any time.

MR. COX: Because you never had any intention of giving her her freedom.

NEILSON: It was the whole point of The Plan to get her free.

MR. COX: Are you saying that the point of The Plan was for her to go free, to give all this information to the police?

NEILSON: The person concerned had no information to give. This is why precautions had to be so strict.

MR. COX: From your point of view, it would be better that

she was dead, because then she could not tell the police anything.

NEILSON: No, sir. It was the exact opposite of what I required. It would be the strongest weapon I could possibly give them.

MR. COX: Supposing you had been stopped on your way back to Halifax on that second day, what would have happened to Lesley Whittle?

NEILSON: If I had been arrested, the only thing to do was to tell them where she was. There would have been no alternative.

MR. COX: The alternative would have been to let Lesley Whittle die and say nothing about it. After all, you read of the heartbreak among the Whittle family afterwards. But did you do anything in the way of a message to them to say where the body was?

NEILSON: No sir.

MR. COX: As you read the newspapers and saw the television, you knew that the drain had not been searched?

NEILSON: There was a deception going on which was obvious to anyone following the news bulletins on radio and television and the newspapers.

MR. COX: I suppose you followed those avidly, didn't you?

NEILSON: I did indeed.

MR. COX: But however hard you read, you couldn't escape the fact that The Plan had failed, and you pushed Lesley Whittle to her death, didn't you?

NEILSON: The Plan did not fail. The girl's death was not my concern. I did not kill Lesley Whittle. My conscience is clear. I disclaim all responsibility for her death.

No further witnesses are called. The case for the defense rests.

.   .   .

The judge has no gavel to make his authority abstract and deafening. He must compete for mastery with the other personalities in the courtroom, and at the same time process all the information produced by the trial. He must preside in all stiff stillness, but register every word said, and discriminate between the versions on offer. The conflict makes him seem sometimes like a bullying secretary, halting the natural rhythms of rhetoric while he writes it all down. At other times he represents his reactions in mime, with abrupt gestures which overcompensate for the inexpressive wig and his physical remoteness from the action. To get the effect of an increase in concentration, he has to lean very far back and look over the rims of his half-moon glasses. The glasses look more like an actor's prop than a genuine corrective; and in fact he must play audience, prompter and critic, for the actors in the court below him.

After the addresses the judge embarks on his summing-up. He occupies the spotlight for many unbroken hours, and there is no-one present to interrupt him as he has on occasion interrupted those arguing before him, no-one to bring him up short. But there is a second, absent audience which he must please, made up of those of his superiors who will consider an application for leave to appeal. He seeks to earn from them the adjectives <u>masterly impeccable faultless</u> for his summing-up of the case. If he makes a mistake, or even a questionable emphasis, the whole trial may be upset. He must avoid any eccentricity, and take good care to explain from first principles the doctrine of <u>reasonable doubt</u> and of the jury as <u>judge of the facts</u>, taking direction from the judge only on points of law. Since no summing-up is correct without these elements, good summings-up tend to resemble each other. A summing-up is judged to be more admirable, the more completely it negates the special newness of its material.

The judge is king in his own court, but from the point of

view of satisfying his second audience, he walks a tightrope. Scope for self-expression is minimal, and the resulting house style is a rhetoric which combines a smooth surface with a fair-mindedness which borders on the neurotic. The judge leads by following, enforces by obeying.

Several times during the summing-up the marshal must warn the judge, by passing a note if necessary, of little blunders which should not pass uncorrected. The judge abbreviates the persons of the case, in his notes, to initials, and frequently slips up when reconstructing them—producing Graveson instead of Grayland, for instance, Shepherd instead of Skepper. To the marshal, the judge resembles the prototype of a machine, which must be nudged now and then to keep it working as it should.

It is an impressive machine nonetheless.

THE JUDGE: You must decide, members of the jury, whether the phrase IF POLICE OR TRICKS DEATH, in the ransom note, constitutes a threat to kill Lesley Whittle. You will ask yourselves, "What happened to Lesley Whittle three days later?" She was dead. She died shortly after the defendant decided, rightly or wrongly, that there was a police trap closing in on him. She died at a time when he was actually getting on the platform to see her. What an astonishing and unfortunate coincidence. It may be said that it was an empty threat, but the fact remains that she died after he realised that the police were closing in on him. There were only two people who could tell you what happened down there, sixty feet underground. One of those persons is dead. In the circumstances, it calls for you to examine the evidence of the survivor with some care. He is in the position of being able to say what he likes about what went on without fear of being contradicted. But there is another side to that coin. If this man is innocent, he has been deprived of the best witness he could possibly have to support his case—the person who could say that he did not push her and wore a mask the whole time they were underground, and who never saw a glimpse of his face. There is no direct evidence that Neilson pushed her off the side. The prosecution case depends very largely on circumstantial evidence, and you must be very conscious of that fact when, in a few moments, I ask you to retire and to consider your verdict. You are here to do justice to this man, not to do something which you think might please relatives, friends, or persons whom you met in a public house. You are here to do justice.

The _marshal_, when he is not occupied with his crossword, is in a position of privilege as compared with the rest of the court. He can observe the judge's presentation of authority without being a focus of it, and he can see human legs supporting the administrative deity. To the marshal, the judge seems as clearly divided as a merman or a centaur. It fascinates him that the judge should so often lift his legs clear of the floor and hold them out in front of him, or swing them gently from side to side. This little repertoire of movements is the only antidote the judge permits himself against the sedative advance of the case. If his face must sacrifice its mobility to the rigours of the job, at least his feet can celebrate their separate existences and keep the whole hybrid organism awake.

The judge's only other trick is to introduce a menthol lozenge into his mouth without being seen by his court. The tiny distention of the mouth round the sweet, and the very slow chewing movements which release the aromatic syrup, are perfectly compatible with judicial attitudes. Only the marshal can detect the faint crackling of waxed paper as a new pellet is unwrapped.

In his chamber, during the court's occasional adjournments and above all during the long wait for the jury's verdict, the judge's manner is quite opposite. Unwigged, he paces the car-

pet with impatience, mopping his face and murmuring variations on the phrases <u>what a terrible case</u> and <u>how that poor
child suffered</u>. These sentiments can have no place in his
running of the case, but he has a need to express them somewhere, and he is as relieved as anyone by the adjournments. He
drinks copiously to prepare himself for the next stretch of
desiccating concentration. Scratching, he further irritates the
area of soreness left by his wig.

The crowd in the court also longs to express itself, and to
endorse the measures taken on its behalf for the protection of
the public. But which is the decisively theatrical moment, the
moment of verdict or the moment of sentence? Which is the
natural signal for the release of tension?

The verdict has come and gone before the public gallery can
properly react to it. A few spectators have time to murmur
<u>good</u>, Neilson himself to mouth a single inaudible word, before
they are silenced by the procedural continuity of the case. For
the lawyers at least, the verdict signals only a change of gear,
the substituting of one pile of papers with another. They are
too busy administering the mystery to consider its audience
overmuch.

Yet from now on the course of the case is fixed. The judge
must listen to pleas in mitigation, but he can pronounce only
the one mandatory sentence for each verdict of Guilty on a
murder charge, life imprisonment; he has no power to moderate or extend it. And so at the moment when he shuts the
defendant away on a permanent basis, he is fully enclosed by
precedent. All the what-a-terrible-case intensity is there in his
voice, but he can choose only the words, not the meanings. He
is striking a retaliatory blow on society's behalf, but his own
hands are tied. All his energy goes into assuring the court that
<u>life</u> in this case must <u>mean life</u>, that parole must not even be
considered for many years to come; but this is not a matter that
he personally will be called on to decide, and <u>I sentence you</u>

to life imprisonment, like I love you, is a pronouncement which is weakened by apparent intensifiers.

THE JUDGE: I am empowered by Parliament to recommend the minimum period which should elapse before you are considered for release. As I understand the law, I cannot formally recommend that you should never be released. But in my judgement, such is the gravity and the number of offenses and the dangers to the public when you are at large, that no minimum period of years would be suitable. In your case, Donald Neilson, life must mean life. If you are ever released, it can only be on account of great age or infirmity.

Neilson turns and runs down the steps from the dock to the cells. A few more goods can be heard from the public gallery, until they are interrupted by a sharp clapping noise from no apparent source. It sounds like slow solitary applause to express irony and contempt, and it comes from the steps to the cells.

Only when they read the papers later on do judge and marshal learn that this is not the message intended. Before being led off to the cells, Neilson breaks away from his escorts to perform a set of the superdifficult clapping press-ups which form part of his fitness regime, and will continue to do so even in prison. In this context, his message turns out to be resolution and not contempt. I am still superfit, Neilson is saying, still a supercrook. No jail can hold me.

MR. GRAY: Throughout this case I have been retained to represent Mr. Neilson's point of view—
MR. COX: —while I have articulated the Crown's version of these offenses. But there is a very real sense—

MR. GRAY: —in which we are more united than divided in our attitudes—

MR. COX: —inasmuch as we both represent the claims of due process—

MR. GRAY: —as against unruly fact.

MR. COX: We share a dislike of untidiness—

MR. GRAY: —and we are accustomed to constructing arguments which are exactly and diametrically opposed. If I use a fact to show Neilson as a ludicrous fantasist—

MR. COX: —then I must use it to show him as an ice-blooded master-planner, or not use it at all.

MR. GRAY: Neither of us welcomes the contradictions of this character—

MR. COX: —since we need him to be pure Jack the Ripper—

MR. GRAY: —or Walter Mitty, one-hundred-per-cent. If he falls between these artificial extremes—

MR. COX: —then there is no voice in the court which will speak for him—

MR. GRAY: —and the confused uncomfortable truth will never emerge. A false polarity set up in court will limit all future speculation.

MR. COX: Neilson had learned in the army, where obsessional thinking is rewarded with promotion, the paramount importance of planning—

MR. GRAY: —but a large part of his planning as a civilian involved anticipating the enemy, and here he was almost always wrong.

MR. COX: From beginning to end he thought of his jobs as military operations and not criminal ones—

MR. GRAY: —but he overrated the opposition.

MR. COX: He needed to show himself superior to the police—

MR. GRAY: —but there was really no contest. They were not in his league.

MR. COX: He worked out that the best force to use against

him would be a pair of SAS troopers with night-sights on their rifles, and using the Starlight night-scanner—

MR. GRAY: —while the police remained strictly at the leg-work-and-public-relations stage.

MR. COX: And he confiscated Lesley Whittle's watch, for fear that she would memorise the times of the trains she could hear from the drainage shaft, and so enable the police to pinpoint her position, after her release—

MR. GRAY: —when in fact very few kidnapped seventeen-year-olds would be thinking along those lines. He assumed his habits of mind were general—

MR. COX: —when in fact all his plans depended on their being unique.

MR. GRAY: He blinded himself with his own imagery. Just because he had devised a plan which needed an athlete's physical skills, a surgeon's impersonal precision, and a commando's logistical daring—

MR. COX: —didn't automatically mean that his project was a sporting event—

MR. GRAY: —or a medical necessity—

MR. COX: —or a bold strike into enemy territory.

MR. GRAY: And he could be tripped up only too easily by the unruliness of fact.

MR. COX: He had planned the kidnap for 1974; and he was flexible enough not to go through with it when difficulties arose—

MR. GRAY: —but not flexible enough to consider how the world had altered, before he put The Plan into operation unchanged in 1975.

MR. COX: His information dated from 1972, when Lesley Whittle was a schoolgirl of fourteen who would be away from home, and needn't be considered in The Plan;—

MR. GRAY: —but by January 1975 she was a student home on her holidays, getting ready to return to Wulfrun College of Further Education in Wolverhampton.

MR. COX: So when Neilson approached the house at Highley, he was expecting to take either Ronald or Dorothy Whittle—

MR. GRAY: —and to leave a ransom note for the other. He would have had no trouble dealing with either; they weren't nice, getting their money from someone who didn't deserve it in the first place. The same ransom note would do for both.

MR. COX: But Lesley was different. She was altogether too much like Kathryn, the fiercest focus so far of his mixed feelings. And just as his love for Kathryn was marred by his need to mould her with discipline—

MR. GRAY: —so also his professional indifference for Lesley held a strong undercurrent of tenderness. He always denied that his interest in her was sexual—

MR. COX: —saying, I have a daughter of my own at home.

MR. GRAY: He just felt protective towards her—

MR. COX: —though he was also the agent of her jeopardy.

MR. GRAY: He tethered her by the neck, but he gave her a long wire as a favour, and he padded the noose with 6 ft. $5\frac{1}{2}$ inches of Elastoplast.

MR. COX: Dorothy would have got less; Ronald perhaps a lot less. And somehow Lesley Whittle managed to make contact with that submerged goodwill, and managed to spend the time while Neilson was away in a state of hypnotised passivity.

MR. GRAY: Even though he caught up on his sleep while he was in Bradford, and displayed his presence insistently to the neighbours, she remained intact.

MR. COX: Although he was away on that occasion for a minimum of ten hours, she was able on his return to read the ransom instructions with the necessary calm.

MR. GRAY: She managed to find, and hold on to, his conviction that no harm could come to her.

MR. COX: But in the process she increased the pressure on him. His schemes were demanding enough as it was—

MR. GRAY: —but when he couldn't make contact with the

police on the first night, he had to keep another person besides himself calm and hopeful.

MR. COX: Plastic puzzles, brightly-coloured napkins, a little music, newspapers and paperbacks, were no real answer to the boredom and fear of a kidnapped seventeen-year-old—

MR. GRAY: —but he did his best. He kept her fed, and he tried, in all ignorance of how to do it, to keep her happy—

MR. COX: —without breaking those rules of his on which her safety depended.

MR. GRAY: Even when the second attempt to start a ransom trail ended in disaster with the shooting of Gerald Smith, he worked hard at reassuring her.

MR. COX: He had been away for fourteen hours. He explained that the tape-recorder had broken down so he couldn't send the message—

MR. GRAY: —but there was nothing to worry about. Luckily, there was plenty to distract her in the tape-recording of fresh instructions, and the preparation of fresh Dymo-tapes.

MR. COX: Finally on the Thursday night he contacted the Whittle house by phone—

MR. GRAY: —and set the ransom trail in operation. He was able to tell Lesley she would be free in a couple of hours, and he started to clear up his equipment.

MR. COX: Her dressing-gown was still wet, so he showed her the clothes he would lend her for her release—

MR. GRAY: —a pair of trousers, socks, a pullover, some training shoes.

MR. COX: When he handed her the shoes (size seven), she said:

MR. GRAY: "These for me? They're huge."

MR. COX: It cheered her up.

MR. GRAY: Then he gathered up his belongings, including the torch, and climbed up the ladder to his rendezvous.

MR. COX: She never saw him again.

MR. GRAY: Since Tuesday she had become good at waiting.

MR. COX: She could hold out for ten or fourteen hours without too much trouble.

MR. GRAY: But no-one entered the drainage shaft for another two months.

MR. COX: And this time she didn't have the torch.

MR. GRAY: She had a gold signet ring and some silver jewellery made for her by her boyfriend. She shared the platform with the ill-fitting clothes lent her by Neilson. She had the sleeping-bag she was zipped up in. She still had the sound of running water, and trains still passed every now and then. But this time, she didn't have the torch.

MR. COX: And this time, she didn't have any food.

MR. GRAY: All she had was a lot of waiting to do.

MR. COX: To start with, Neilson was waiting too; he was waiting above the drainage complex for the ransom messenger to arrive. But he was tense and wound-up in his waiting, poised to take quick and effective action when his schemes had their final testing; while to start with at least, Lesley's waiting was calm and passive.

MR. GRAY: Neilson set up one torch, the one with the Dymo message, in the floodwater spillway, and flashed a second one at the only car which came near him—

MR. COX: —but it contained a courting couple, and they paid no attention to him.

MR. GRAY: Police procedure slowed down the ransom messenger, police inefficiency confused the trail. But in Neilson's mind were two SAS troopers—

MR. COX: —with night-sights on their rifles, using the Starlight night-scanner. So when he saw a helicopter nearby—

MR. GRAY: —and heard the barking of dogs—

MR. COX: —he <u>knew</u> the police were closing in on him—

MR. GRAY: —and he ran in panic down from the mound he was standing on—

MR. COX: —down towards the disused railway line. He fell down—

MR. GRAY: —dropping his holdall and spilling its contents. He took it for granted that the police were right behind him.

MR. COX: In fact they were some considerable distance behind, and in disarray. Ronald Whittle didn't arrive for quite a time. Then he drove slowly past the shaft where Lesley was held, and on down the track. He did his best to abide by the ransom arrangements, but it was too late for that.

MR. GRAY: It wasn't too late for a search of the Park, but nothing was done that night.

MR. COX: Very little was done next day. The Yard men weren't keen on squandering their expertise on a routine search—

MR. GRAY: —while West Mercia felt the Yard people should take the rough with the smooth, and not guard the Yard mystique, the Yard glamour, so single-mindedly.

MR. COX: Some detectives poked around the Park a bit, and found nothing.

MR. GRAY: They were confident they knew all there was to be known about the Criminal Mind. It had few twists and turns, and all were clearly labelled. It wasn't a labyrinth, hardly even a cave. At one stage the detectives even held a briefing session on top of the shaft—

MR. COX: —but they failed to recognise the sheer scale of Neilson's deviance—

MR. GRAY: —and they failed to discover the size and extent of the tunnels under Bathpool Park.

MR. COX: Much of the warren was disused and not shown on maps, and the search stopped almost before it began.

MR. GRAY: Policemen are fond of maps.

MR. COX: Neilson had counted on the police forces to be parochial, petty, insular and reluctant to share information among themselves—

MR. GRAY: —but they exceeded his estimate on all these counts.

MR. COX: And meanwhile Lesley Whittle lost, among other things, weight.

MR. GRAY: The tether in the tunnel had been Neilson's compromise between too much mobility, and a claustrophobic confinement (binding and gagging) which he felt would have severe mental repercussions.

MR. COX: But Lesley Whittle, tied up to the ladder and left, was not quite mobile enough to escape mental repercussions.

MR. GRAY: Her state of mind showed deterioration.

MR. COX: Stomach cramps alternated with periods of numbness.

MR. GRAY: No light reached the platform, sixty feet below ground.

MR. COX: Starvation is notably bad for the sense of balance. Desertion is bad for the sense of proportion.

MR. GRAY: And at some stage, after a minimum of two days in the dark (gastric evidence), Lesley Whittle got bored with her horizontal position—

MR. COX:—and without leaving the sleeping-bag which was saving her from hypothermia or pneumonia, struggled to her feet—

MR. GRAY: —(in the process sweeping her release-outfit of borrowed clothes into the canal)—

MR. COX: —perhaps gave the wire clamped to the ladder a last few affectionate tugs—

MR. GRAY: —and fell off her platform.

MR. COX: The sleeping-bag saved her neck from injury against the rusty lip of the landing, but slid from around her when she was brought up short by the wire.

MR. GRAY: She is unlikely to have noticed the snagging stanchion without which she would have landed on her feet, with inches of wire to spare.

MR. COX: Certainly there were no rubbing marks on toes or feet to indicate that she struggled to raise herself—

MR. GRAY: —and vagal inhibition has a lot to be said for it, when starvation is the alternative.

MR. COX: She had lost weight and was very thin.

MR. GRAY: Her stomach and intestines were completely empty.

MR. COX: In court, the prosecution explained this by suggesting that Neilson never fed her at all, that the story of buying fish-and-chips, chicken-legs, of making soup, was a heartless lie spun by Lesley's captor to excuse himself, that she ate for the last time on the night before the kidnap—though the voice on the tapes was a fed, relatively content voice—

MR. GRAY: —while the defense maintained that she was fed, and simply ignored the discrepant fact that her stomach should then contain significant traces, if she died when Neilson claimed.

MR. COX: Neither side canvassed the untidy truth.

MR. GRAY: Even Neilson was slow to see it. He went on thinking he had had a lucky escape, and he was amused by the simple-mindedness of the newspapers.

MR. COX: They said Lesley Whittle was still missing, and expected him to believe it!

MR. GRAY: There was a deception going on which was obvious to anyone following the news-bulletins.

MR. COX: But once again he overestimated the power of the police. Nothing easier, he thought, than suppressing information, and setting traps with the connivance of the media.

MR. GRAY: And because police and Press in their different ways championed the public good, he assumed they were working in harmony.

MR. COX: So he played the waiting game. He could play it as well as anybody; he had waited a year to do the final job. The cat had beaten the dogs enough times before.

MR. GRAY: Only when news came of the body being found did he have doubts.

MR. COX: Then he studied the reports as never before.

MR. GRAY: And finally he had to realise that it was true. The additional details—

MR. COX: —Lesley's arms pinioned by her sides, a drop length of forty-five feet, the word <u>death</u> scrawled on the underneath of the shaft lid—

MR. GRAY: —established the reports as bona-fide journalism.

MR. COX: Just after the discovery, someone called the Manchester office of the Guardian and admitted responsibility for the post-office raids—

MR. GRAY: —but the caller insisted again and again that Lesley Whittle's death had nothing to do with him. But there were many bizarre calls arising from the kidnap, and this one got no special attention.

MR. COX: The whole business hurt Neilson much more than anything ever had. He didn't like to think about it.

MR. GRAY: But when he said to Detective Chief Superintendent Robert Booth, "<u>You killed her, not me</u>"—

MR. COX: —it wasn't just a cliché of post-arrest rhetoric.

MR. GRAY: And when he came to make a statement, he preferred to suppress the truth for his own peace of mind.

MR. COX: He wasn't going to confess to a murder he hadn't committed—

MR. GRAY: —but in his version he could at least compress Lesley's sufferings into a few seconds.

MR. COX: And so he constructed a death-scene from the accounts he had read in the papers.

MR. GRAY: The newspapers then, which had supplied so much information, true and untrue, timely and untimely, in the course of the case, at last supplied him with details of Lesley's death, and then reported them all over again, when he reproduced them in his testimony in court.

MR. COX: A more alert court would not have let his version pass—

MR. GRAY: —since it failed to mention the sleeping-bag, or the snagging stanchion which made a fatality of what would otherwise have been a mere bruising accident. These elements were missing from the reports in the press. Nor did Neilson make mention of the inevitable twitching, the likely swinging on the end of the wire.

MR. COX: And then again, the strangeness of his emphasis should not have gone unnoticed.

MR. GRAY: How many men, after all, when accused of murder, would place all their stress, not on the statement I didn't kill her, but on the insistence that she was dead before I left?

MR. COX: Of course she was dead before he left, if he pushed her off the platform as the Crown maintained. But he was rejecting an internal suggestion, not one from outside. You left her there to die was the accusation he feared, not you murdered her. But the crucial suggestion was never made in court.

MR. GRAY: He could stand the idea of beating a middle-aged woman until she was unrecognisable—

MR. COX: —but the idea of deserting Lesley Whittle was intolerable to him. Only once in the whole trial was he able to call her Lesley Whittle and not her or the girl. He couldn't undo the fact—

MR. GRAY: —all he could do was make sure it never appeared on the record, and eventually erase it from his mind.

MR. COX: Neither view of Neilson presented in court could accommodate this action of his. It wasn't quite the callous lie of a master-planner—

MR. GRAY: —but nor was it the confused confession of an unfortunate fantasist—

MR. COX: —and no intermediate complexity could come to light in court.

MR. GRAY: Neilson's willed rewriting of painful events, for instance—

MR. COX: —had the effect of obscuring the crucial part played by police inefficiency and the wilfulness of the Press—

MR. GRAY: —over and above its original intention of salving Neilson's conscience.

MR. COX: The trial, not for the first or only time, channelled blame rather narrowly.

MR. GRAY: It is no part of the court's duty to investigate police procedures.

MR. COX: That's a pity.

MR. GRAY: And so police and Press conspired unknowingly with an unknowing criminal—

MR. COX: —to kill a girl whom everyone wished well (each after his own fashion)—

MR. GRAY: —and then an unknowing court conspired with a defendant who wished to forget—

MR. COX: —so that no full story should appear.

MR. GRAY: A bargain was struck by the forces of law and order—

MR. COX: —without their even knowing it. Established structures acted to spare themselves—

MR. GRAY: —and passed up the chance to investigate their own flaws.

MR. COX: In this respect the legal system acted as a nervous system rather than a brain.

MR. GRAY: Its unsuspected priority was to continue functioning, not to establish truths—

MR. COX: —at the risk of its own safety, by exploring its own procedural underpinnings.

MR. GRAY: It will be a good long time yet before such a system is able to recognise an element of real conflict beneath apparent collaboration—

MR. COX: —between West Mercia and the Yard, Press and police, defendant and defense, truth and law—

MR. GRAY: —and a level of collaboration beneath the supposed conflicts—

MR. COX: —of prosecution v. defense, Panther v. police, R. v. Neilson.

MR. GRAY: It is, after all, the legal system's achievement to split up its actions so that they belong to no one person, and amount to a decision of the community—

MR. COX: —it isn't exactly the judge who sends the defendant to prison, nor exactly the jury—

MR. GRAY: —while on a smaller scale, just this atomising of responsibility was the secret of Neilson's criminal psychology.

MR. COX: An authoritarian outlaw, tabulating the laws of crime, he confronted the established order with its parody.

MR. GRAY: No tears need be shed for Neilson. If he was slightly innocent of Lesley Whittle's death, he was guilty enough of the postmasters' to earn the sentences he is serving in Leicester jail.

MR. COX: His psychology seems to raise the question: "If the contest is between energetic deviance and a comatose authority, which is it that we should choose? Is order more of a threat than the threats to order?"

MR. GRAY: But that is to overrate Neilson's deviant energy.

MR. COX: What could be more wooden as planning than to attack a household in 1975, as if it was still 1972?

MR. GRAY: And what could be more unthinking than to familiarise yourself with a house—

MR. COX: —climbing the staircase again and again until you had the creaks under control—

MR. GRAY: —and never to doubt that it's a millionaire's mansion, never to notice that it's little more luxurious than your own? The most that we can say of Neilson is that he chose his trance.

MR. COX: He invented his disease.

MR. GRAY: And he is quite certainly where he belongs.

MR. COX: But can the same be said of anyone else involved in the case?

MR. GRAY: None of them was dealing from a full deck—

MR. COX: —though perhaps the whole story, viewed from all angles, is a full deck.

MR. GRAY: Tout comprendre est tout condamner—

MR. COX: To understand all is to condemn all—

MR. GRAY: Tout pardonner n'est que rien comprendre.

MR. COX: Universal forgiveness is the sheerest ignorance.

A knock at the door is the signal that the official car is ready and waiting outside the court. The judge has been relaxing in his chamber without the burden of his wig, but now he must put it on again. Two policemen are waiting outside the door, one to head the little parade, the other to bring up the rear.

Though the judge is the senior member of the procession, and the reason for its existence, it is impractical for him to set the pace. Its leader must do that. In this case, as the judge and marshal are already moving and in step with each other, the adjustment involves awkwardness. With a tiny lurch and a series of half-steps, the judge synchronises himself with the policeman striding confidently ahead of him down the corridor. The marshal and the second policeman must then reproduce this stumbling dance, if they are to be impressively co-ordinated when they enter the crowded hallway of the courtroom. The second policeman, who has picked up the marshal's step a fraction before it is modified, has the hardest time of it.

For a few moments in the corridor they resemble a second-rate mime troupe pretending to trip on a loose floorboard. Then they sweep into the open, and are on show.

The massed reporters make another barely successful bid, with their respect and their orderliness, for the judge's attention. He rapidly returns to looking ahead of him.

The judge manages to crunch up his last lozenge before his party reaches the top of the steps and is photographed.

The brightness of the street is shocking after so many hours spent in gloom. The judge screws up his eyes against the glare, and the expression caught by the cameras is one of wizened disapproval. The marshal, bending forward so that he will fit into the car without awkwardness, is recorded as a hunched and flustered figure as he emerges into the unenlightening brilliance of the afternoon.

Photographers are again perched on the low wall outside County Hall, and jostle each other with undiminished fierceness. The crowd cheers and applauds, singing a raucous version of For He's a Jolly Good Fellow. The official car pulls away behind the escorting bikes. A preceding police car stage-manages its escape from traffic.

Between court and lodgings the judge is in limbo; he is no longer on full display, but ritual dress continues to exclude him from any real relaxation. He maintains the stiffness of his pose all the way to Shotover, long after he has passed from the notice of the public.

When the convoy arrives at Shotover, the butler moves smoothly from the doorway to greet the judge and relieve him of his carried gloves. The more intimate act of unwigging is reserved for the hall. The marshal drops his hat and wilting gloves on the hall table.

Judge and marshal are now free to change into dark suits. They have a couple of hours' leisure before dinner, which they spend rereading the newspapers and watching television. A snippet of film showing them emerging into the light is screened on the early-evening News. It has been running for some seconds before they recognise themselves.

The marshal would like to walk into Wheatley and sample the local beer, which is brewed by Morrells and has a good reputation; but he would have to inform so many people of his movements, for reasons of security, that the pleasure would seep out of the project.

Judge and marshal dress for dinner, though they are not entertaining company. The heat makes a further set of formal clothes an unappealing prospect; but any other costume would fall short of the dining-room's expectations, and it would pain the butler to exceed his employer in formality.

Conversation at table is fluent enough, but hardly lively. It is part of the marshal's job to keep things moving along without asserting himself too forcibly, and to hold himself ready for the judge's hints that one subject be dropped and another explored.

After dinner it is the judge's pleasure to walk in the grounds and feed Rodney the swan. His cook sets bread aside for the purpose. The judge describes this walk as a refreshing break from the day's routine; but it seems to the marshal that since they divert themselves identically every day, their expedition is itself routine. Certainly for him it involves remaining in his role, and even observing some new courtesies. He responds with enthusiasm to the judge's praise of the grounds and house itself, and the Greek Temple, and the Gothic Temple at the end of the lake; he knows he mustn't divert Rodney's attention from the judge's bread with his own.

The greedy, elegant swan stands out very white in the diminishing light. The two follies cannot compete with it for brightness.

But the Gothic Temple at least, viewed from across the water, has the celebrated effect of concentrating the sun's near-horizontal rays and beaming them against a central niche bare of statuary. While the judge and his marshal look on, this glowing shell of golden stone holds the gathered rays, and seems to refine them to an almost tangible focus of brightness; until the light drains off underground.

A NOTE ON THE TYPE

The text of this book was set via computer-driven cathode-ray
tube in Avanta, a film version of Electra, a typeface designed by
W(illiam) A(ddison) Dwiggins for the Mergenthaler Linotype
Company and first made available in 1935. Electra cannot be
classified as either "modern" or "old-style." It is not based on
any historical model, and hence does not echo any particular
period or style of type design. Electra is a simple,
readable typeface that attempts to give a feeling
of fluidity, power and speed.

Composed by The Haddon Craftsmen, Inc.,
ComCom Division, Allentown, Pennsylvania
Printed and bound by The Haddon Craftsmen, Inc.
Scranton, Pennsylvania

Designed by Judith Henry